THE MAN FROM HELL

Borgo Press Books by JOHN RUSSELL FEARN

THE MAN FROM HELL

CLASSIC SCIENCE FICTION STORIES

JOHN RUSSELL FEARN

Edited by Philip Harbottle

THE BORGO PRESS
MMXII

THE MAN FROM HELL

FIRST EDITION

Published by Wildside Press LLC

www.wildsidebooks.com

DEDICATION

To the Memory of Rick Minter

CONTENTS

ACKNOWLEDGMENTS

These stories were previously published as follows, and are reprinted by permission of the author's estate and his agent, Cosmos Literary Agency.

"The Man from Hell" was first published in *Fantastic Adventures*, November 1939. Copyright © 1939 by John Russell Fearn; Copyright © 2005 by Philip Harbottle.

"Mark Grayson Unlimited" was first published in *Thrilling Wonder Stories*, Spring 1945. Copyright 1945 by John Russell Fearn; Copyright © 2012 by Philip Harbottle.

"Science from Syracuse" was first published in *Science Fiction*, March 1941. Copyright © 1941 by John Russell Fearn; Copyright © 2004 by Philip Harbottle

"White Outcast" was first published as "Mystery of the White Raider" in *Fantastic Adventures*, February 1940. Copyright © 1940 by John Russell Fearn; Copyright © 2012 by Philip Harbottle.

ABOUT "THE MAN FROM HELL"

BY JOHN RUSSELL FEARN

I suppose stories about atomic force are legion. I know I can recall them over a period of fifteen years in sf mags, and since *The World Set Free* in books. But how many such stories, with the exception of *The World Set Free*, really covered all the likely territory of such a fascinating subject?

Actually, "The Man from Hell" is a combination of two original ideas. The first idea was "How much would a man learn if he passed over the gulf of death and, by some scientific process, came back to life?" That set me wondering. Suppose, say, Aristotle had gone on adding to his knowledge in the Hereafter? How much would he know now? A good deal, I figured— so I worked it into the yarn. It does, I know, set the reincarnation theory at discount, but it is as logical as reincarnation (and one must have two sides to a question), so I used it.

Another idea that linked up with this was a statement by Sir Arthur Eddington in his *New Pathways in Science*. He says at the close of his brilliant chapter on

"Subatomic Force"—

"It cannot be denied that for a society which has to create scarcity to save its members from starvation, to whom abundance spells disaster, and to whom unlimited energy means unlimited power for war and destruction, there is an ominous cloud in the distance though at present it is no bigger than a man's hand."

Now, suppose that handsized cloud came right overhead? What of the struggles of men to use this power for all its worth? That gave me the idea of big business operating unscrupulously to utilize this mighty discovery of a young scientist. Because he hindered big business, he was callously destroyed. Up to here I had the logical human slant on the problem.

This might develop into an ordinary story of atomic power, I thought. But no plot is new; it is the angle that counts. So, what if the dead man returned to claim his secret, and not only claim it, but to use it for powers never dreamed of? What if atomic force is really only one of several doors to power? Suppose its mighty strength is not limited to just the release of energy?

I have tried to piece together theories old and new and knit them up into a yarn of interest with human characters going back and forth across the background. In consequence, to achieve the balance of action in the first parts, I have shuffled between the characters with episodic swiftness in order that the interest may not flag at the wrong moment. I hope I have succeeded.

As to the end, some may be disappointed—bit I must say in justice to myself that I considered it the only possible finish. I could have invented a high-powered scientific miracle to make things happy ever after, but is there not a certain realistic poignancy in the vision of an empty beach down which the conqueror of unrest passed for the last time? I have a feeling there is. It is for you to judge.

EDITOR'S NOTE
by Philip Harbottle

The foregoing essay was written by Fearn (under his 'Polton Cross' pseudonym) for the 'Introducing the Author' department of the November 1939 issue of *Fantastic Adventures* magazine, in which his story first appeared. Another essay (under his 'Thornton Ayre' pseudonym) for the same magazine appears later on in this collection, for his 1940 story "White Outcast."

At the time "The Man from Hell" was written, the storm clouds of war were gathering in Europe, and atomic power had yet to be released—though secret research was being carried out by the governments of the leading world powers. But whilst his story is of course now outdated, it remains thought-provoking, and its power and entertainment value is undiminished. I considered it an ideal story to lead off this new collection of Fearn's classic stories from the sf pulp magazines.

At the time it was published, the story made an immediate impact, as evidenced by editor Ray Palmer's announcement in the January 1940 issue of his magazine:

PRIZE STORY CONTEST

"For the first time in our prize story contest, a single story has ran away from the rest. We are proud to announce that Polton Cross, authoring 'The Man from Hell' in our November (1939) issue, has gained our readers' complete approval, and really earned himself that $75.00 first prize. Congratulations, Mr. Cross, on an exceptionally popular story. Come again—say we, and our readers!"

"The Man From Hell" garnered 2,759 first-place votes, giving it an average rating of 80% amongst voters. The general approbation for the story was reflected in the magazine's Reader's Page letter columns:

"I have several reasons for selecting Polton Cross's story for the best. The major one is the ending. I applaud an author who is not afraid to portray real life and use common sense in ending his story not quite so perfectly for all concerned. Not that I'd like all stories ending unhappily, but one like this is really refreshing. One kept expecting the hero to be saved miraculously at the end when he speaks of a desperate experiment, and it comes as quite a shock that he does not survive.

"When I began this story I feared that it was another of those 'atomic power' things, and was relieved that the author introduced his spatial power—something different. I think it presents interesting possibilities.

"My third reason is that I think the number one story ought to live up to the name of the magazine—and if a man returning from the dead isn't fantastic, I don't know what is!"— *Barbara O. Shryock (Penna.)*

"It seems to me that no other story in your magazine could portray such adventures in the field of atomic power, combined with a glance beyond death, as 'The Man from Hell,' by Polton Cross.

"The very title of your magazine is portrayed in this story by the fantastic adventures of Dake Bradfield."—*Donald F. Campbell (Iowa.)*

The flow of positive comments was carried forward into the letters pages in the February 1940 issue:

"*What is beyond the great divide?* Surely that is a question that everyone is, of necessity, interested in. Mr. Polton Cross, in his story 'The Man from Hell,' in the November issue of *FANTASTIC ADVENTURES*, has quite a lucid theory.

"'The Man from Hell,' besides being a fast moving story, packed with action and drama, deals with another subject that is of universal interest.

"Scientists all over the world have been experimenting with atomic force. Who knows—perhaps in our lifetime the dream of governing atomic power will be realized.

Mr. Cross has dealt with these subjects in a quite interesting manner, and, for having done so, gets the nod from this umpire for having the best and most interesting story of the issue."— *Claude W. Williford.*

"There's an old saying that a story is not a story if it hasn't got an idea behind it. Therefore, a story with a good idea behind it is considered an acceptable story. But imagine a story with three swell ideas behind it, each one good enough for a book-length novel! 1: 'Return from the Dead.' 2: 'The Danger of Atomic Force.' 3: 'Salvation of the World.' A title like 'The Man from Hell,' and an author like Polton Cross. What a combination! There you have my reason for selecting this as the best story of the issue."—*Harold Topf (New York.)*

The praise came not only from ordinary readers, but also from one of the leading scientific experts and commentators in the field:

"First place in the November issue goes, in my opinion, to Polton Cross' story 'The Man from Hell.' It is a very good imaginative tale, slightly off the usual type of science fiction stories (I mean, leaning a bit toward fantasy, but not much) but still convincingly written.

"The important point is, I think, that this story...proves that the present-day political set-up practically excludes a good number of possible scientific discoveries. It makes me wish that certain scientific discoveries—especially that of releasing the energy of the atom—may be delayed by a kindly fate until humanity is ready for them."— *Willy Ley (New York.)*

This latest collection of Fearn's vintage short stories follows *Dynasty of the Small*, and has been especially compiled for The Borgo Press. Further titles are in preparation!

THE MAN FROM HELL

CHAPTER 1
MURDER!

"Gentlemen, atomic power is ours! As you are all aware, I lodged with Dr. Carson yesterday the results of my five years' research into the mysteries of atomic power. For next to no cost we can provide every city in the world with light, heat, and power.... And note these words, gentlemen! We have in our hands the greatest power man has ever known. It is born into a world crammed to the doors with diabolical armaments of every description. We all know how disastrously the attempt at world disarmament of 1970 ended. It is up to us to defy temptation. We must overrule the lust for barbarism and keep in check the desire for world-control which atomic force could certainly give us. I give my discovery to the world that it might benefit the world.... No more, no less."

Dake Bradfield stopped speaking, his powerful hands resting on the broad table on the speaker's platform. Then he stood upright, hands going to his hips, massive dark head thrown back. His piercing blue eyes passed swiftly over the faces of the hundred men gathered before him. For a moment he was conscious of the supreme power he represented. He of all men, son of a scientist, still only thirty-six years old, had done what all other men had failed to do—mastered the mystery of atomic power. His firm lips curved in a smile.

"I have nothing further to add, gentlemen," he stated quietly, and sat down amidst a roar of applause.

But Dake Bradfield was not concerned with the eulogy: he was trying to efface from his mind the possible consequences of his discovery. Again he wondered if a world stalemated with arms was a safe place into which to bring atomic power. But the thing was done now! The formula was in the hands of Dr. Carson, respected President of the Scientific Research Association. Only he, Bradfield, and Elford—Secretary General to the Association—knew what the formula was about. But suppose there was a slip-up somewhere—

This was thinking too far ahead! Dake Bradfield forced his thoughts to the moment; he was glad when the convention was at last over and he could escape outside into the great marble corridors of the Association Building.

He looked round eagerly amidst the swirling variety of people, nor was he disappointed. Presently, a slim, auburn-haired girl in trim walking costume disentangled herself from the delegates and pressmen and came forward.

"Dake, you are marvelous!" she exclaimed, her dark

eyes shining in admiration. "I heard it all over the relay speakers, of course. You predicted you would knock them cold—and you did! I'm proud of you, dear."

Dake smiled, drew her arm through his. "The opinions of Sheila Carson matter more to me than all the vaporings of delegates," he murmured. "If you think that, your father must think so as well. And since your father is my boss, it sort of works out."

They walked slowly along for a moment or two down the hall, then Dake spoke again.

"If every guy in the world had a girl like you to help him, we might have less bitterness," he sighed. "Did you ever stop to think that you've wasted the best part of your life waiting for me?"

Sheila wrinkled her nose. "Well, you said you were too busy to marry me and settle down—and since you've proved your point now, what does it matter? After all, our marriage is an insignificant thing compared to the discovery of atomic force...." She broke off suddenly and gave him an indignant glance. "Say, what do you mean—wasted the best part of my life? I'm seven years younger than you, remember. I'm no faded blossom yet!"

"Nope, I guess not," Dake amended. "Only I think sometimes I've been a bit of a heel making you wait. But now it's all finished with," he went on intensely, his blue eyes shining. "We'll be married tomorrow! We'll take a honeymoon for a vacation. God knows I need one!"

"Tomorrow! But—but—"

"Special license. And no arguments! The best way to celebrate my success is to marry you. Now let's go and grab a bite to eat."

They turned away swiftly towards the dining rooms, unaware that the expressionless eyes of Elford, Secretary General to the Association, watched them go. Elford turned, a small and impassive enigma of a man, and walked unhurriedly out of the building.

* * * * * *

On the topmost floor of the gigantic Brant Steel Corporation Building in the heart of New York reposed the sumptuous office of Marvin Brant himself, President of the Corporation, multimillionaire, autocrat, and quasi-dictator of America's teeming millions of average workers.

At the moment Brant was pacing his office very slowly with his plump hands locked behind him. He was a bullock of a man with vastly wide shoulders and the face of a champion bulldog. His hair, though thinning, was still raven black, an excellent testimony to the iron strength of body that had lifted him from a smelting foundry to consummate power and wealth.

He paced his office as though be were alone, ignoring the man seated in the hide chair by the door. Not that the man seemed to mind. He smoked a cigarette leisurely and stared at the ceiling meditatively with steely bright gray eyes.

At last the desk buzzer sounded. Brant stopped his perambulations and snapped the switch.

"Well?" His voice was thick and husky, matching the folds of his heavy, pallid jowls.

"Mr. Jones to see you, sir."

"Send him right in."

Brant stood expectantly waiting, his keen eyes on the office door as 'Mr. Jones' came in. It was Secretary Elford. He glanced at the man in the chair, gave a calm nod of acknowledgment, then advanced to the desk.

"You heard and saw everything over the radio-tele-vizor?" he asked the big man briefly.

"Naturally. What we're waiting for is your verification. Has this fellow Dake Bradfield really got atomic force?"

"No question of it," Elford replied in his level voice. "In the hands of the Science Association is the greatest power this world has ever seen, power which could have broken you down utterly, Brant, had you not had the wit to foresee what was coming."

The magnate's smile had no humor in it. "I sure had the right hunch when I engineered you the job as the Association's Secretary. In five years you have become installed as the essence of honor. It has been well worth the wait. Naturally, you know where this formula is?"

"Do I!" Elford echoed, his pale eyes shining. "As the Secretary, Dr. Carson handed it over to me. It is entirely in my hands, and all you have to do, Brant, is pay me the sum agreed upon and the formula is yours. There are no copies of it, except in Bradfield's own brain. Once I have taken the formula, I shall vanish from the Association and team up with you— But I needn't say any more."

"No...," Brant whispered.

He sat down at his desk, rubbing his big paws together in grim exultancy. "At last we have it! Atomic power! What can we not do with that formula? I need it to save my own interests, yes—but we all need it for domination of the Earth. You, Van Rutter, will use it for the creation of atomic shells, with which you will load our hidden air fleet in Europe...."

The man in the hide chair inclined his dark head. His lean, ascetic face was smiling twistedly. Henrich Van Rutter, of nationality unknown, was more than an arms magnate: his interests went beyond even the ruthless probings of Marvin Brant. But the two were inseparable because they knew each other's power.

"You, Elford, will take control of my own munitions and science laboratories under this very building," Brant went on, turning to the Secretary suddenly. "You'll be safe enough. Nothing can get into my laboratories, nothing. And every man is to be trusted. Between us we can master the Earth."

"Has this atomic force invention been tested by anybody else save Bradfield as yet?" asked Van Rutter sharply.

Elford shook his head. "He has given demonstrations, but our own scientists have yet to go to work. Bradfield's formula shows how to release atomic force for commercial purposes, but he has withheld the secret of how to make explosives from it. Not that that signifies anything: our scientists will soon discover what to do. That, I believe, has been Bradfield's main fear all along."

"Bradfield," said Brant slowly, "must disappear. I have it all arranged. As you know perhaps, Bradfield does not live in the city here. He prefers the privacy of a little isolated house two miles outside the metropolis. To reach his house he has to cover three miles of unmade road. That very fact makes him mainly immune from interference, for an automobile cannot comfortably go along that road. Few people ever use it at all, in fact. Bradfield, my agents tell me, walks to and from his house every day to the city, probably for exercise. Tonight he will never reach home. He will be killed on the way."

"And what if the shot is heard?" Elford asked quietly.

The big man scowled. "Who in hell said anything about shooting? Give me time to finish, can't you! Bordering this unmade road on one side, in the midst of undeveloped land, are old mine workings. You remember the radium search in 1950 when some nut figured he'd found radium near here? Well, those disused workings are the result. Ultimately our friend Bradfield's body will be thrown down one of the mine-shafts. But first he'll be strangled to death—sound-lessly and efficiently. For that I shall engage my old friend Vanson, the one-time Manhattan Strangler. He's a crook anyway, ready for the hot seat any time I say the word. He'll do any job for a reasonable sum."

"And if the police track it all down?" Van Rutter questioned.

"Can you imagine the police being very interested in the disappearance of Dake Bradfield when all their energies will be directed on trying to find a stolen atomic force formula?" Brant asked with calm cunning. "And even if they do get ambitious, I can always find a convenient maniac to take the rap. Money can buy anything. It's better we use a common or garden way of killing Bradfield than anything elaborate. The more ordinary it is, the more suspicion is deflected from us, even granting there is any at all. It's all so simple, gentlemen."

"Yes—I think you're right," Elford admitted finally.

"O.K., then, the rest is up to you. Get that formula!"

* * * * * * *

Dake Bradfield's mood was a happy one as he swung along that solitary country road between the metropolis and tiny garden city suburb where he had elected to make his home. He had left Sheila Carson in the city with a promise of an early arrival on the morrow. Then, at last, their long-delayed marriage. Afterwards, the South Seas, Paris....

Dake whistled as he strolled along, hands thrust deep in the pockets of his navy blue overcoat. A cold full moon shone through lowering autumnal clouds.

In the field to his right beyond the barbed wire fence reared the broken skeletons of the mine workings, relics of a brief period when man had thought radium was on his doorstep. Now it was atomic power: but that was no dream. It meant the start of a new age, an age of—

Suddenly Dake stopped in his tracks, conscious of a faint sound in the clinkered dust behind him. He twisted around, but at that identical moment something thin and strong dropped lightly round his neck and instantly drew taut. With a frantic desperation he lashed out at the massive form he could sense behind him.

His efforts were useless, not because he lacked strength, but because he was at a disadvantage. Besides, that damned cord was crushing the wind out of his lungs. He pawed air helplessly, gulped and gargled, dropped heavily to his knees.

Tighter the cord constricted, and tighter. Dake felt his lungs turn to liquid fire: the moon span crazily before his eyes. Darkness swirled in upon him in a singing tide....

Vanson, the Manhattan Strangler, waited a while with the cord still in position, then at last he stooped and felt for his victim's heart. It had ceased to beat.

Vanson smiled, pulled the cord away, and thrust it in his pocket. For several seconds he stood looking down on the dead, tortured face in the moonlight.

"The easiest pay-off I ever earned," he commented thoughtfully, then humming a tune to himself he lifted Dake's heavy body onto his broad shoulders, ducked under the barbed wire fence, walked steadily across the empty field toward the nearest mine working. At the top of the first shaft he stopped, released the body, and stood listening.

Some seconds afterwards there floated back to him from the bottom of the shaft a faint squelching thud, announcing Dake had landed in the heavy mud at the bottom.

Vanson dusted his coat with calm movements, re-adjusted his hat, drew on loud yellow gloves as he strolled languidly back to the deserted roadway.

CHAPTER 2
Sheila Makes a Discovery

The following morning scare headlines blazed across the front of nearly every American newspaper—

ATOMIC FORCE SECRET STOLEN!
INVENTOR DISAPPEARS!

Then the full résumé of facts, including the disappearance of Secretary General Elford from the Association. Had he too been killed and disposed of, like Dake Bradfield?

The police were suddenly thrown into desperate activity, working in collaboration with the Intelligence Service—but Brant had laid his plans well and diverted every lead into a blind alley that led nowhere. Certainly nobody suspected the steel magnate. He had, in the five years at his disposal, prepared for every possible eventuality. Nor for that matter did anybody doubt the character of Elford. It was presumed he had met a violent and mysterious end in common with Bradfield.

Dr. Carson, slim, gray-headed chief of the

Association, was at his wits' end with worry. Upon him rested the sole responsibility for the theft. It would mean ruthless enquiries, accusations, probably the loss of his position for negligence, though God knew it had not been his fault. The whole business was an utter mystery to him.

To Sheila the news had come as an overwhelming shock. This day should have been her wedding day, the happiest of her life, was the cruelest of all. All through the morning she remained in something approaching a daze, then toward noon she bestirred herself far enough to dress and go down town to see what events had transpired.

"Nothing—nothing at all," her father told her drearily, once she was within his private office. "Frankly, my dear, though you know my heart goes out to you in your own sadness, I am far more concerned over the theft of that formula than anything else—"

"It's Dake I'm thinking of!" Sheila broke in with sudden fierceness. "He's got to be found, dad! Maybe he's been kidnapped or something. I just can't believe he's dead: it's too awful.... Oh, what am I doing just sitting around talking? I—"

"Listen, Sheila—please!" Carson came round to her looked earnestly into her tear stained face. "Dake s fate is only a small one when weighed in the balance with that formula theft. Do you not realize that it has fallen into the hands of an unscrupulous power? The very method of its theft shows that. There are no copies of that formula: they were to be made today, and Dake is the only man who knows all about it. He didn't even reveal the nature of his experiments to me. Oh, don't you see? There can even be war unless that formula is found! Dake's disappearance is matched against the possible slaughter of thousands of innocent people. Only a handful of police are engaged on trying to locate him and Elford. As for the rest of the police, they're all looking for that formula. You must understand the situation, Sheila."

The girl nodded slowly, her lips tightening. "I understand all right, but the only thing that matters to me is Dake. I'm going to investigate for myself! I'm going over every inch of the route he must have taken to get home after leaving me last night. I'm going over every inch of the route he must have taken to go home after leaving me last night. I've got to find him, dad! He means everything in the world to me."

"But Sheila, there may be danger—"

"I'll risk it!" she retorted stubbornly, jumping to her feet. "I'm not waiting for the police, or for anybody. I'm starting right now!"

Carson relaxed as he watched her go. He knew it was useless to argue. She was too much like him for that.

* * * * * *

In the immense laboratory of Marvin Brant, completely hidden from the world and safe from attack under the Brant building itself, protected by five-foot walls and ceiling of concrete and steel, white-smocked technicians worked with steady industry.

They had worked in relays through the night ever since Elford had brought in the formula at midnight the previous evening. Marvin Brant himself, sullen with impatience, wandered around the hot hive of industry, understanding little and condemning much, while behind him strolled the impassive Elford and alert Van Rutter.

"How the hell much longer are you going to be?" Brant demanded at last, stopping before a thin-lipped scientist with a broom of black hair sprouting from his big head.

The man glanced up from studying an equipment of globes, vacuum tubes, and projectors. He gave a taut smile.

"I think we're ready, Mr. Brant. The actual production of atomic force is achieved by etherial waves, which are generated by vibration projectors. These incorporate a certain wavelength which shatters the molecular structure of matter and increases the—"

"Be damned to that!" Brant snorted. "I'm no scientist. How do we make bombs? That's what I want to know!"

"It won't be difficult," the scientist responded. "A shell made of copper can be fitted with a small detonator apparatus. The moment the detonator impacts with anything, it will momentarily release the required vibration through the shell, which will of course transform into free energy. I have the men making a small shell and detonator right now. All they want is the exact wavelength for incorporation in the apparatus. I think I have it. I've rigged up this makeshift projector to find out."

"Then get busy, man! What are we waiting for?"

The physicist nodded to the tiny grains on the receiving plate of the apparatus. "I'm going to disrupt those," he said briefly. "If Bradfield's calculations are right they will explode with plenty of violence. But the plate underneath will be untouched. I have got an insulating current running through it You see, there is a wavelength which can protect as well as destroy, and—"

"Endicott, I pay you to show results, not to lecture," Brant broke in, with ominous calm. Then he glanced at the reddish dust in some perplexity. "You don't expect to get anything from this, do you?" he demanded. "What is it, anyway?"

"Copper dust." Endicott smiled grimly. "I fancy you will be a trifle surprised. Just stand back—all of you." He glanced across at the other technicians. "Ready, boys?"

They nodded, and got their distance. Endicott closed knife switches, his eyes on the receiving plate. Brant watched uneasily as the multiple tubes glowed brightly, as the lenses of the roughly erected projectors shone with unholy luminance—

Then suddenly all the men were slammed back against the wall by a blinding flash of light and stunning concussion. Noise struck deep into their eardrums, scorching wind singed their eyebrows and hair.

When finally the balls of fire had receded from before their eyes, they found themselves staring at an apparatus in total ruins, a mass of twisted girders and broken plates.

"My God, what power!" Brant whispered. "It's unholy! You actually mean, Endicott, that that explosion came solely from that copper dust?"

The scientist nodded: he was looking thoughtful. "We've got the wavelength all right, but we've also proved something else. I had hoped we could devise an atomic force projector to disrupt cities on the death-ray principle, but this shows it cannot be done. The projector itself shatters. Bradfield had a system of his own for manufacturing a metal impervious to the release of atomic force with which he intended to build generating plants. Those details are not given in the formula."

"I don't want projectors anyway: I want bombs," Brant breathed, clenching his fists. "I want the power to smash a city with one bomb, to hold a threat over the world. Eh, Van Rutter?"

"I am wondering," the arms king said, "where you intend to drop an experimental bomb? I presume it will be from an airplane?"

"Naturally." Brant gave a triumphant grin. "I have been planning again. We could drop our bomb in the ocean, only it might attract attention. Suppose though we dropped it near, or even on the mine workings where friend Bradfield met his death? Those old workings blow up now and again from fire-damp. One explosion more would not be considered strange, and at the same time we'd eliminate all traces of Bradfield, who is lying, so Vanson told me, at the bottom of shaft number one. Simple, isn't it? And quite deserted around there too."

"Depends on the size of the bomb," said Elford, with a significant glance at the shattered apparatus.

"About half an inch in diameter," Endicott remarked. "That will be ample for a test. Now I know the wave-length, I can have it finished in another three hours."

Brant gave a slow nod and looked at Elford. "See to it that a plane is ready m three hours," he ordered. "A small bomber from my own flying ground will do. To carry four...."

* * * * * * *

It was late afternoon when Sheila Carson reached the lonely road leading to the garden city suburb. She walked slowly, watching keenly as she went, but the landscape remained undisturbed. On one side of her was the high grass bank: on the other the field with the mine workings. Footprints there were none: the road was too full of hard ruts and clinkers for that.

For half an hour she wandered on. An hour went by— Then she paused, having covered perhaps a mile and a half in the time. Her gaze fixed itself to a piece of fabric clinging to the spike of the barbed wire fence bordering the mine field. In another moment she snatched it free, turned it over in her hands. Blue cloth? She recalled Dake's overcoat of the night before.

With a racing heart she looked around her, then finally toward the mine workings. Stooping, she eased herself through the fence and raced across the intervening stretch of muddy field, following as she went the heavy imprints of a man's boots. Heavy because he had carried somebody? It was a hunch far closer to truth than she realized.

But when she reached the mine workings it was a different matter. The skeleton towers of wood and steel loomed all around her. There were monstrous pyramids of disgorged earth, treacherous seams, and crevices. She moved warily, calling as she went.

"Dake! Dake! Oh, *Da-ake!*"

That there was no reply did not deter her. One by one she looked down the deep shafts of the abysmal mines into the darkness at the bottom, until she picked up the footprints again and found them leading to a shaft somewhat separated from the others. With a vague giddiness rolling round her head she peered into the pit, hesitating. She knew she had found the right shaft, that Dake was possibly at the bottom of it despite the fact there was no answer to her call. But had she the nerve to venture down there, alone and unaided by rope?

It was as she stood there debating that a beating hum crept into her ears, growing steadily louder. In vague surprise she glanced up, frowning as she studied a small fast bomber flying directly over the mines, circling to keep them objectified. Though she was already practically concealed by the mine's tower, some inner premonition warned her of danger. Gently she moved into the massive shadowed protection of a girder, stood watching interestedly.

She did not have to watch for long. Unexpectedly, she seemed to be suddenly flung in the midst of hell! The world in front of her opened up in blinding fire as the clear field just beyond the workings was riven with explosion. She was flung off her feet and hurled backward like a rag doll, landed face downward amidst earth and rubbish, her ears singing with the roar of the concussion. Heat and choking fumes swept round her. Earth and stones came down in a deluge, most of it prevented from falling on her by the solid mass of the tower. Then the world was silent again, silent except for the drone of the plane.

Sheila moved slowly, raised her face, and looked cautiously about her. Where open field had been was a crater some twelve feet wide and perhaps eight feet deep. She got slowly to her feet, wiggling her fingers in her ears to clear them again. With weak knees she tottered forward, stopped at the edge of the working and stood well concealed, watching the airplane come swiftly to earth near the crater. It taxied for a moment, then the pilot reduced the engine to a tick.

"Marvin Brant!" Sheila whispered incredulously to herself, as the first figure climbed through the opened doorway. She would know the steel magnate anywhere. She pressed herself into deeper concealment as Secretary Elford followed. Van Rutter and Endicott she did not know: but in any case she had seen enough.

"Lovely! Lovely!" Brant's thick, ecstatic voice carried quite clearly in the still air. "From a bomb half an inch wide we got this! Just think what a one-ton bomb could do! Van Rutter, we can master the Earth! We've got everything tied up in bows."

There was silence for a moment as the group studied the crater, then the plane's pilot came ambling forward. Brant swung on him suddenly.

"Say you, why the hell didn't you drop that shell right on the mine shafts as I told you? According to Vanson, Bradfield's body is in that first shaft there. Why didn't you drop the bomb on it?"

"Sorry, Mr. Brant. I guess the thing was so darned tiny I had my aim all wrong."

"O.K., maybe we'll try again later," Brant grunted.

"We'd better get out of here," Van Rutter remarked abruptly. "Some of those people from the garden city will start blowing along if we don't. We can say we saw the explosion happen, of course, but I'd sooner keep in the clear. Let's go. Satisfied, Endicott?"

The scientist nodded. "Quite. I know now that these bombs will smash earth, rock, and metal. The rest is simplicity itself."

The men turned back to their plane. Sheila remained in her position, watching as the plane started up again. Only when the plane had climbed far into the sky and disappeared toward New York City did she dare to move. Her eyes were narrowed bitterly.

"So it was Elford who stole that formula—for Brant! All right; now we know what to do."

Springing from her concealment she hurried across the field to the road as fast as her still shaky legs would take her. Half an hour or so later she was in a taxi being whirled to the Science Association.

Dr. Carson listened in grim silence as she told her story. If he needed any proof at all, the girl's dirt-caked clothing and frantic eyes were sufficient.

"...so Dake's down the first shaft," she finished hoarsely. "Vanson is a wrestler or something: I've heard of him before. Dad, we've got to get Dake to the surface. By myself I dared not try."

"No, of course not." Carson compressed his lips. "So it is Brant at the bottom o(all this, eh? It's one thing to know he is responsible, but decidedly another to prove it!"

"But—but I saw him and those others drop that bomb! At least we can have Vanson arrested."

Carson shook his head slowly, his face serious.

"Brant is the most powerful man in this city. You can be assured that Vanson is under his protection. He'd get him freed instantly. We're dealing with a man who is utterly ruthless, Sheila. He can crush you, and me, the whole Association, without effort. No, we've got to think very carefully before we act. However...." Carson got to his feet briskly. "I'll notify the authorities and let them worry over it. For our part we'll get over to the mine with equipment right away. While you get changed I'll gather the boys. Be ready in fifteen minutes."

* * * * * * *

In his own office Marvin Brant was smiling complacently as he regarded Elford and Van Rutter.

"You know what to do, Van Rutter?"

"Of course." The arms man thoughtfully regarded the photostatic print of the atomic force formula, then slipped it in his brief case. "I'll have every available factory in my European ring working at full pressure right away. After that it is simply a matter of loading the planes with bombs. Five hundred planes carrying no insignia are already waiting at the European underground base."

"Good!" Brant's eyes gleamed. "You, Elford, will work in conjunction with Endicott and set to it that bomb manufacture goes right ahead. We go into action in seven days...."

CHAPTER 3
THE PHANTOM AVENGER

The autumn dusk was closing down when Dr. Carson, Sheila, and the workmen arrived with their mobile van at the mine workings.

Carson remained silent as the girl pointed toward the crater in the dying light, then she turned eagerly and flashed on her torch, pointed to the heavy footprints leading to the first mine working.

Carson stared into the black, windy depths and stroked his chin. Then he glanced around the landscape.

"Better lay off the searchlight for the moment, boys:

we don't want to attract attention if we can help it. O.K., Hurst, let's get started."

The gang boss nodded, signaled to his boys. Between them they slung a thick rope out into space, fixed it quickly to a pulley, let the free end hang over the shaft. Followed a snapping of clips and a cradle was in position.

"I'll take it," said one of the men briefly, a broad shouldered giant in corduroy. He settled himself in the cradle, switched on his torch, then gave a nod. The winch on the truck started to unwind the rope slowly.

Leaning as near the edge of the shaft as they dared Carson and the girl watched anxiously as the torch light went bobbing into the emptiness below. It became remote, vanished at last as the man's body presumably hid it from sight.

"He's a long time," Carson said at last, uneasily—then the words were no sooner out of his mouth than from the shaft there came an unearthly, echoing scream—a scream of mortal anguish followed by heavy silence.

"Say—what in hell was that?" whispered the foreman huskily.

"Pull him up—pull him up!" Carson panted, recovering himself suddenly. "Quick, man!"

Instantly horny hands tugged on the rope winch handle. After twelve turns the dead weight in the cradle came sprawling like a sack of coals over the shaft edge. It was the laborer all right, gasping and choking heavily.

"What's the matter, man?" Carson shouted, seizing

him. "What went wrong down there?"

The man breathed erratically, swallowed air in great gulps.

"Something—something horrible down there, Doc. Like—like bayonets going through my heart. I guess— I fainted—"

"Was Dake Bradfield there?" Carson demanded.

"No—the shaft's empty...." The man stopped, made a twisting motion, then relaxed. In horrified silence the group glanced at one another. Then Hurst stepped forward and took the man's pulse.

"He's dead, chief," he said soberly, glancing up.

Carson's jaw set. "A man of his strength killed by something we do not understand, and no sign of Dake in the shaft. Listen, Sheila, either you were wrong in what you heard or—you are quite convinced you heard Brant say that Vanson had thrown Dake's body down this shaft. You are sure you saw Brant, Van Rutter, and the rest of them?"

The girl nodded wearily. "Of course! Let's have the searchlight down the shaft. We should have done it at first."

Carson nodded to the waiting Hurst. The dead man was gently lifted onto the truck, then the searchlight swung into action, poured its blazing beam down the shaft. Motionless, the party gazed to the bottom of the length. The light reflected slightly from soft mud.

"There are ruts all the way up the shaft," Hurst remarked at length. "A guy *could* climb up—"

"Don't talk rubbish!" Carson snapped. "Dake

Bradfield was dead."

"But suppose he wasn't?" Sheila put in quickly. "That soft mud would save him from injury if he fell slackly."

Carson stood brooding. Hurst said, "Well, he ain't there anyway. What's next, chief?"

"I wonder what he means by bayonets through his heart?" Carson's keen eyes wandered to the position of the bomb crater in the darkness.

"You boys stay here," he said suddenly. "Kill that searchlight and wait for me. I'm going back to head-quarters for some instruments. Whatever killed Mason must have a scientific explanation, and I think it just possible that bomb crater may have something to do with it. Come Sheila."

He turned swiftly towards the car parked next the truck.

* * * * * * *

Vanson, the Manhattan Strangler, put the finishing touches to his bow tie, patted his tuxedo in satisfaction, then turned from the dressing table mirror. Humming through his heavy, scarred lips he walked briskly into the comfortably furnished layout of the drawing room. This uptown apartment did not match his personality, but what of it? It was a good joint to bring a blonde to.

He turned to the wall-safe, twisted the combination wheel, took out a wad of currency.

"All this for bumping a guy off with a piece of sash cord," he said slowly. "Brant sure pays well for service—and did he get good service!" He flexed his vast shoulders, stuffed the notes in his wallet, then glanced at his watch. In ten minutes he was due to pick up Daphne Gibson. Then—

He grinned in anticipation. Daphne wasn't too tough when a guy with money wanted to do a spot of necking. Supper uptown, then back here....

Humming leisurely again, Vanson shut the safe and ambled over to his hat and coat, put them on with the air of the gentleman he fancied he resembled. He moved to the main door, then stopped at a sound behind him. Slowly he turned to look at the cause of it—and if Vanson had never known fright in his life before, he certainly knew it now.

A motionless figure stood in the doorway leading to the bedroom—a figure in a torn, clay-caked suit, a figure with dark hair trailing down over his ashy, merciless face. There were eyes watching from that face, eyes that did not blink, eyes of piercing blue that took account of every move. The mouth was one straight line, unyielding and inflexible.

Slowly Vanson's horrified gaze traveled to the apparition's hands. They were level, and apart, holding a length of sash cord between them.

"Dake Bradfield!"

The words belted from Vanson's lips by the sheer force of the terror behind them. He stumbled backward for the door, fumbled with the knob, fished for the key. The door was locked, being the outer one, and somehow that key failed to work in his paralyzed fingers. All the time he kept his eyes fixed on that figure. He could feel sweat pouring down his face.

"Why did you kill me, Vanson?" the figure asked at last, in a cold, brittle voice—and at the same time he advanced with soundless tread, the cord dangling from his fingers.

"I—I didn't!" Vanson shouted hysterically. "Now listen, get this straight! Give me a break, can't you?"

"You killed me, Vanson, for money from Brant," Bradfield said, in the same dead, level voice. "I heard you say so when you took your money from the safe. I came through your bedroom window. You killed me, Vanson, and now I'm going to kill you. Simple, is it not?"

"But—but you can't! You died! I—"

Vanson broke off and made a dash for it, but that was his undoing. The cord dropped suddenly round his bull neck and pulled taut. He twisted, lashed around with a ham of a fist, but another like the bumper of an automobile crashed into his jaw and sent him reeling.

He fought helplessly against relentless, overpowering strength. His muscles seemed like putty against the man he had killed. This strangling cord.... As he reeled into darkness he saw that gray, unsmiling face watching him.

Bradfield left the cord where it was round the Strangler's neck, went out silently the way he had entered.

* * * * * * *

It was midnight before Dr. Carson finished his experiments with a battery of instruments at the mine working. His face was perplexed in the light of the moon.

"I don't understand it!" he declared worriedly. "The instruments show that some kind of powerful radiation is prevalent in the bottom of the shaft. But it doesn't fit into any classification I know of. I thought at first it might be the emanations of radium, that there might really be radium deposits down there. Now I realize I am wrong."

"Then Mason got the full force of this radiation?" Hurst asked quickly.

"Yes: none of which explains where Bradfield has vanished."

"What—what do we do now?" Sheila asked anxiously.

"What can we do?" Carson turned disconsolately to the car. "All I can do is turn these instruments over to the Association for examination and see if they can analyze anything. The police will have to try and solve the mystery of Bradfield. Come, my dear. It's no use standing moping here. Besides, we're in danger all the time we stop here. Brant and his men might come along— All right, boys, pack up and let's get home."

Sheila turned slowly away, too miserable to speak a word.

* * * * * * *

Henrich Van Rutter stirred uneasily in bed, aware of

a distant strident noise. By degrees wakefulness came to him: he switched on the light and squeezed his eyes at the telephone, lazily lifted the receiver.

"Well?" he yawned into the mouthpiece.

"Van Rutter? Say, something terrible's happened!" The urgent voice of Marvin Brant at the other end of the wire was sufficient to spur the arms king into alertness. He stared at his watch—2:20 a.m. What the hell did the big fellow want at this hour? And as he thought, he listened.

"...and Vanson has been killed, strangled with a piece of sash cord. It's serious, Van: somebody's onto our plans."

"Needless worry," Van Rutter growled. "Probably some pal of that ape's that had a grudge against him—"

"Then why was he strangled in the same manner as Dake Bradfield?" Brant demanded. "Suppose Bradfield didn't die after all? I only got the news a little while ago. A dame called Daphne Gibson rang up and asked me for help. She was found at Vanson's apartment and the police are holding her. I'll help her, of course. She wouldn't have the strength to strangle Vanson anyway."

"And what now?" Van Rutter asked, with ominous calm.

"We've got to hurry things up, Van. You were planning to start for Europe tomorrow, weren't you?"

"Correct. Everything to be ready in seven days."

"We've got to alter that," Brant said grimly. "You must leave for Europe within the hour, and we want action before seven days. How soon can you make it?"

"I can have a hundred bombs manufactured by sundown tomorrow if I get my factories on double shift. A hundred can do plenty of damage for a first warning. The rest can follow for the attack proper."

"O.K.!" Brant sounded relieved. "Hop to it, and let me know how you make out. I'll increase the shift on my own production too."

Van Rutter hopped out of bed, yelled hoarsely for his manservant....

At the other end of the wire, Brant sitting up in bed like a vast porpoise in a vividly striped pajama suit, dialed another number with frantic haste.

"Elford?" he snapped, as that calm voice answered him.

"Yes, Mr. Brant. Anything wrong?"

"Plenty! I have an uneasy feeling that Bradfield isn't dead after all. I've no time for details now; I'll tell you tomorrow. Where's Endicott?"

"Home. I'm supervising the shift."

"Get Endicott and tell him the shift's doubled. Press every available scientist into action. We want bombs in half the time we planned. Understand?"

"Right!" Elford rang off without further questions.

"Good man, Elford," Brant muttered, lying back on the pillow and meditating. "Knows how to keep his trap shut."

He switched the light off and composed himself for slumber again. But somehow he could not doze off; his mind was too active at this sudden upset in his plans. He opened his eyes again and lay looking at the long oblong of moonlight cast through the unshaded window.

It was perhaps fifteen minutes later when he saw the moonlight dim before a shadow—the outline of a man's head and shoulders. He lay rigid, listening, heard the window catch slide back gently. Through his eyelashes he watched a figure jump softly down into the moonlit area and stand watching him.

Stealthily, Brant's hand crept under his pillow and dosed on the revolver that always lay there. Then in one movement he whipped the gun level and fired— the figure did not budge for a moment, then it came through the smoke of the discharge, switched on the bedside lamp, and stood glaring down with unholy calm.

"Bradfield!" the steel man gulped. "Then my guess was right!"

Bradfield said nothing, but his hand shot out abruptly and whipped the gun from Brant's hand, sent it spinning across the room. That done, he wrenched free the telephone wire from wall and phone and swung it gently between his hands. Brant lay watching with his eyes popping.

"At your orders," Bradfield said slowly, "Vanson strangled me with a piece of cord and threw me down a mine shaft. For something like fifteen hours I was dead! *Dead!* Then I came back to life. How, is my business. Of all the men that have ever died, Brant, one came back—and that one is me! I have many things to do, but vengeance comes first. I have killed Vanson; I shall kill you. Then Elford, then Van Rutter. One by one!"

"Wait!" Brant exclaimed, his jowls quivering. "I'll give you back the formula. It hasn't been used yet." He thought swiftly of Van Rutter's photostatic copies. "I'll—I'll give it back to you and five million dollars in cash. That's a fair bargain!"

"You consider that fair recompense for seeing beyond the grave?" Bradfield's voice contained an awful, chilling solemnity.

"Ten million then—anything you want!" Brant was sweating visibly.

"Anything?"

"You have only to name it!" Brant cried, hope flooding his ashy visage.

"Very well, I will. I want your life!" And with that Bradfield's hands suddenly shot out and whipped the telephone cord round the magnate's neck. It tightened with irresistible force.

"Now you know how I felt, as I died," Bradfield whispered. "It got tighter—and tighter, like this, until...." He left the cord knotted and watched the final threshing of the gross form amidst the bedclothes. That empurpled face with its starting eyes was not a pretty picture.

"At this moment it is a cleaner, sweeter world for being without such as you." Bradfield spoke to the dead man calmly, then he glanced up at a sudden hammering on the door.

"Mr. Brant, are you all right, sir? I heard a shot a few moments ago. Mr. Brant—"

Bradfield turned, glanced toward the buried bullet in the window frame whither Brant's lightning aim had sent it, then he moved to the window and slid out gently into the night.

"Van Rutter...," he mused as he dropped to the grounds.

* * * * * *

The newspapers next morning carried a conglomeration of news, most of it under the heading of—

MARVIN BRANT MURDERED

All over America people read of the magnate's death at the hands of an unknown slayer. The parallel case of Vanson was quoted, but not played up.

Some people were sorry to hear the news—Brant's financial friends mainly—but everybody was disturbed by the hints contained in the general write-up.

> "...and according to our European representative's information, received only an hour ago, the death of Marvin Brant will have wide repercussions. It is not even improbable that International complications may develop between this country and Europe. Henrich Van Rutter, the eminent arms king, hinted at possible complications in an early interview this morning when he landed at Paris airport to attend to

financial matters precipitated by Brant's death. It is thought...."

So it went on, until most Americans realized that the death of Marvin Brant was to mean far more than just that. His interests were so far reaching, so complex.

Sheila Carson, haggard from a restless night, burst into her father's office during the morning, waving the newspaper in her hand.

"You've read this, dad?" she asked breathlessly, and he nodded gravely.

"Long ago, over breakfast."

"It's Dake!" the girl cried, her eyes wide. "I— I can sort of feel it inside me. Brant and Vanson both died the same way as Dake, and since we couldn't find Dake it proves—"

"It might prove that the man who murdered Dake also murdered Vanson and Brant," Carson said quietly, then at the girl's troubled look he came round the desk and gently put an arm round her shoulders.

"You've got to think clearly, Sheila," he went on gravely. "Don't get hysterical notions because you want them to be true. I realize what you're thinking— but I've been thinking a bit longer than you. It cannot be Dake, because he was killed, and nobody can come back from death. Certainly this strangler has done us a good turn by killing Brant—but there's an even more dangerous enemy in Van Rutter. In the newspaper it says he went to Europe to settle Brant's affairs. Brant, according to the police, was strangled at 2:40 this morning. Van Rutter, however, caught the 3:00 a.m.

express airliner for Paris. He could not have known of Brant's death when he started off, as he'd have us believe. He must have got news over the radio as the plane flew and altered his story to match up with it to Europe.

"So why did he *really* go to Europe? An arms king does not go there at such frantic short notice without grim meaning behind it. We can assume he has the atomic force secret in his possession, that he went under the orders of Brant. All of which means trouble with a capital T. For one moment I dared to suspect that he had killed Brant, until the time discrepancy showed he couldn't have done it in the time. The airport authorities cleared that up very quickly."

"Elford, perhaps?" Sheila mused: then she shook her head firmly. "No, dad, it was Dake! Call it intuition, but I'm convinced—"

She broke off and waited as the desk buzzer sounded.

"Well?" Carson said brusquely

The girl's voice in the outer office was nearly a whisper. "There is a strange man out here who says he must see you, Dr. Carson. He has got sticking plasters on his face and dark glasses. Says the name is Mr. Brown."

"Brown?" Carson frowned. "Oh, send him away. I'm too busy right now to—"

"He says he can tell you about Marvin Brant."

"He can! That's different. Show him in...."

Sheila and Carson stood watching curiously as the individual with the dark glass and long overcoat was admitted. He waited until the door closed, then swiftly locked it. Rapidly he pulled off his soft hat, glasses, and plasters, revealed his face in all its ashy whiteness.

"Dake!" Sheila screamed, springing up "Oh, Dake, thank God you're safe! I—I—thought—"

"Quiet!" he commanded, as she flung her arms about him. "I don't want to give myself away. I'm just Mr. Brown."

"I don't care who you are—you're safe," Sheila whispered, then she looked up in surprise as he pushed her gently away.

"Not now," he said shortly. "That can come later—"

"So you were not killed after all?" Carson asked levelly.

"Well, of course he wasn't!" Sheila exclaimed. "What more proof do you want than him standing here? Dake, you—you look ill. Did you hurt yourself getting out of that mine?"

He hesitated briefly, then said, "No, I guess not. That does not matter right now. My worry at the moment is that Van Rutter got away. I killed both Vanson and Marvin Brant last night, but when I went for Rutter he was missing. I've found since that he went to Europe. I might never find him there. Neither can I get at Elford, deep under the Brant building."

"Then you knew Brant was the one who tried to have you killed?" Carson said.

"I knew the facts from you and Sheila. When you were at the minehead I was close by; I heard all you had to say."

"You let us go to all that trouble!" Sheila exclaimed, amazed. "That wasn't very—"

"I had no time to explain then," Dake broke in. "I set out to find Vanson and Brant. I may as well tell you I'm alarmed. From the morning papers I believe Van Rutter had some orders from Brant before I strangled him—and from the trend I'd say my stolen atomic force is going to plunge us into devastating war before many days have gone by. To find Van Rutter or Elford now and stop them is impossible. The only other course is to defeat this attempt at domination by scientific means. I only hope to Heaven I have the time."

"Time? For what?" Carson frowned.

Dake gave a start. "Nothing—just something I was thinking about." He looked at the pair steadily. "I know you're puzzled by all this, but you're going to be even more puzzled when I tell you that I was strangled. I died. For fifteen hours I lay dead at the bottom of that shaft, and then—*I returned to life!* I cannot describe it. It was both horrible yet fascinating, like awakening from a long adventure in a strange land."

He stopped. Father and daughter were staring at him blankly.

"It—it isn't possible!" Sheila stammered, white-faced.

"It happened," he said gravely. "And while I was dead I saw and heard so many things. Learned so much. Some day you will know...." He stared in front of him: for a moment he was a man apart.

Then Carson said slowly, "Is it possible that that

atomic bomb crater had anything to do with bringing you back to life?"

"Maybe." Dake listened attentively as the doctor went through the story of Mason's strange death and the ultimate recordings of the instruments.

"Is it possible," Dake mused, "that atomic force has other powers of which we never even dreamed? The power of life and death? While I was dead I gained knowledge, enough knowledge to work out all the powers of atomic force, given time. Since you made instrument recordings, the task won't be so hard. My return to life must have had something to do with that bomb. I'll find out...if I have the time."

"Dake, why do you keep saying that?" Sheila asked, stirred by an uneasy premonition.

He did not answer. Instead he said, "We must prepare, Doc. I want the full run of the laboratories to put certain ideas into effect. The staff will help us whilst maintaining secrecy. We face a very real danger from Van Rutter. Strange indeed if the dead defeat the living! For such it really amounts to."

He turned, donned glasses and sticking plaster again.

"I'm waiting, Doc. How soon do we get down to the lab?"

"Now," the scientist answered quietly, and glanced in mystification at the girl. He fancied he saw a faint horror in her eyes, a horror that her waxen smile could not entirely hide.

Death had changed Dake Bradfield in some subtle, unexplained way. He was unquestionably a man from

Beyond. And marriage? The very idea of it seemed completely forgotten.

CHAPTER 4
CATACLYSM

Paris saw them first, against the wild autumnal sunset. Out of the silence of that fateful October evening came a low droning note, at first attracting no attention, then gradually establishing itself in the senses as a very definite thing—the roar of airplane engines. The frontier posts of France, always manned became sudden hives of industry. Alarm gongs rang throughout the mighty entrenchments of the Maginot Line.

Fifty unknown airplanes heading toward Paris in V-formation from the direction of Russia! By radio the news flashed to Paris headquarters. Possibly undeclared war from somewhere! The reports became an expanding ball of frenzied warning reaching to all parts of the world.

Russia, the mighty, the mysterious, evolving unknown plans through numberless years, had decided to strike. The planes must be Russian. The planes of every other country were recognizable. Paris waited, warned in five minutes of the approaching horde. Not very many people were concerned. Possibly it was a trial flight by somebody or other; somehow frontier laws had been violated. As for a possible attack, nobody believed it. The French authorities went about the task of demanding inquiry from Russian headquarters.

Air-raid warnings sounded in Paris. Anti-aircraft guns swung to the defensive. Searchlights penciled through the twilight. If it was a mistake, it would be good training, anyway— But it was no mistake! In another fifteen minutes, flying at bombing height and with a velocity making them difficult to catch with the hastily manned guns, the planes arrived.

No air raid in military archives, no earthquake in history, could match the fifteen minutes that followed. Three shells dropped simultaneously and Paris lifted right out of the earth! Endless miles of brick, steel, and concrete lifted in crumbling ruin to the skies, fell back in a thundering deluge of debris. High quarters, low quarters, business, and suburban regions. The whole lot went up in blinding explosive fire under the impact of atomic force. Nor did it end there. A cataclysm followed as the English Channel raged over the ruptured land and pounded a new coastline where Angers and Dijon had formerly stood.

The horror, the incredible violence of those bombs, was something defeating imagination. Three bombs, no more, and half of France ceased to exist. There were no survivors. The people were destroyed before they realized what had happened to them. And those of other countries who had felt the earthquake concussions only had a glimpse of planes returning toward Russia as genuine night began to fall.

The world waited, stunned. But the wait was not for long.

* * * * * *

At 10:00 p.m. a radio call on an unknown wavelength swamped the frantic yammering of newscasters. A voice spoke with clear-cut decision. England heard it, and America, and in other countries interpreters went to work. Hardly anybody in the world did not hear that voice.

In the laboratories of the Science Association, Bradfield, Sheila, Dr. Carson, and the assembled scientists stood listening in grim silence.

"I address this communication to the respective Governmental heads of every country in the world. All of you have seen what happened to France. That country, as a country, has ceased to be. I have power such as no man has ever known before. I can destroy, ruthlessly: but I can also build. I have no intention of destroying anything further for the pure sake of it. France was used as an example. Here is my ultimatum—

"Each country individually will resign its existing form of government and surrender unconditionally to me. Who I am will be revealed in due course. You may rest assured that my rule will be one of progress. If my ultimatum is accepted, agents will make themselves known at a specified time. They will complete the legal negotiations. If the ultimatum is refused, remember France!

"You have until midnight on Wednesday, four days hence, to decide. Broadcast your decision: I shall hear it. A last warning—any attempt to find me will result not only in the destruction of the investigator, but in the annihilation of the country he represents That is all. Think carefully."

The communication ceased. Dake reached forth his hand and switched off, then gazed on the morose assembly.

"Obviously Van Rutter," Carson said finally.

"And if that massacre he pulled in France is any guide, he means it too," Sheila exclaimed. "He must be an idiot, though: he might know that no Government will accede to a demand like that. The world is armed to the teeth anyway. There'll be the most unholy war over it."

"Four days," Dake mused. "I just wonder if it's possible for me to do it in the time?"

"Do what?" Carson's voice was clipped with impatience. "Even if we manufactured similar atomic bombs, we'd only create havoc just as bad. He's got us cornered, Dake."

The scientist paused as he saw Dake smiling, that cold infinitely superior smile.

"There are some things about atomic power which Van Rutter does not know," Dake said slowly. "And there are some things about science which I never knew—until I died. I thought when I had found how to release atomic force that I had discovered the mightiest of powers. But what I learned beyond death showed me that I had but unfastened the first of many doors, leading to deeper and more formidable forces, basic universe strata."

Involuntarily Sheila Carson gave a little shiver.

There was something eerie, overpowering, about the inhuman calm Dake radiated. There was something frightening in his constant reference to after-death experience.

"Just—just what are you getting at?" Carson questioned.

"I found spatial power...."

"Seem to have heard of that some somewhere." Carson thought for a moment. "Theoretically, of course. It was Soddy, in his *Matter and Energy*, who said there might be another power of which we know nothing, from which electricity and other forces are merely offshoots."

"You're right," Dake said, with a quiet nod. "The first man to moot spatial power was Aristotle. But Soddy slightly enlarged on the original theory."

Carson laughed shortly. "Some use that is! Aristotle's been dead for centuries—since around 400 BC!"

"Did you ever stop to think how much his mind could have progressed in the time that has passed since then to the present day?" Dake asked quietly. "I met Aristotle—out there. I met them all—the ancients and moderns who have died—Sir William Barrett, Henri Bergson, Archimedes, Nicolas Carnot, Copernicus. Their bodies died, some recently, some centuries ago, but their minds have lived on, progressing into the vast forever. While I was dead I met them, found that the theories of each one had reached fruition in positive fact. But to them there was no way back with their knowledge: it was knowledge for space and eternity alone. To me, for reasons yet to be unearthed, life was given back again—and with it much of the knowledge of the men I met."

There was an awed silence. Dake smiled reflectively.

"And I thought I was clever! To be clever, one must die."

Suddenly he seemed to lose his thoughtfulness and went on quickly, "Much of what Aristotle originally theorized you will not remember, but you will recall some modern scientists' elaboration of his theories. Some of them have said that one dominant radiation, or force, constitutes the entire universe. In its essence it is ether, but in its variable states—created by opposing and lesser forces streaming through its midst—it is altered slightly to form into matter, energy of tabulated sorts, life, and intelligence, all different expressions of the *basic* power, but none of them having that basic power's efficiency. No man can ever know what force *is* unless he understands what *ether* is, for ether is the father of force. In the beginning, there was only this streaming force. Opposing radiations created the planets and suns of the universe, begot that ultra-sensitive radiation known as thought, which commingled with matter and gave it life."

"You mean," said Carson slowly, "that space itself, the vast emptiness of the void, is really a mono-force, and that everything else is a warp in it?"

Dake nodded. "All scientists know of the theory: it was left to me to see it as a fulfilled practicality beyond death. It is the answer to power unlimited. It is the key to the universe, beside which atomic force is like a dry battery compared to a powerhouse. What we call empty space actually possesses unbelievable power. And, even as certain radiations warped that space and coalesced to produce matter, so can other radiations destroy the coalescence and bring empty space back to its normal position. It was Einstein himself who said that matter is a pucker or rumple in otherwise clear space.

"Matter can be removed by using the counteractive wavelength that formed it in the first place. It was built up by wavelengths, and can be broken down by the same process."

"And you think you can do this?" Carson asked unbelievingly.

"I know I can, because I have the knowledge of the dead. And when I have done it I shall first remove the Brant building and all its underground laboratories from the face of the universe. I shall make allowances for atmosphere and nothing more. Without fuss or disturbance, the Brant Building will give place to clear air! Then I shall find Van Rutter."

"How?" Sheila looked puzzled.

"Atomic force gives off radiations which are detectable by a compass, even as ordinary radium gives itself away. It is certain that Van Rutter will have some measure of free atomic force in those concealed European laboratories of his. I'll find him."

"You are sure this idea has an advantage over atomic bombs?" Carson mused.

"Certainly. You saw what happened to France. Atomic bombs means ungovernable power—and I mean ungovernable. In making sure of two enemies, we might destroy thousands of lives and create billions of dollars' worth of damage. Sheer force is our weapon. Besides, I have other uses for atomic force later—and other uses for even deeper principles of science."

"Sounds all right to me," Carson admitted at length, "even though I don't figure out how you're going to do it. What will you use for the power to generate these wavelength radiations of yours?"

"Atomic force!" Dake smiled. "A use for it which Van Rutter could never have found—nor any earthly scientist for that matter, unless he died and returned. From a tank of water I can generate enough power for my purposes, power which will pass through circuits and transformers until it has the wavelength, which my mathematics will show as necessary to correct the particular matter-warp we are aiming at. The rest will be simple."

"But how long will it take?"

"It must take no longer than three days. It can be done with all of us working at full pressure The instrument itself will be no larger than an ordinary searchlight. In the meantime, Doc, get in touch with the President, and advise him to contact other countries and tell them to ignore the radio ultimatum, and to keep all news of such activities from the general public so far as is possible. All we need, outside laboratory work, is a plane to be converted to transparency on all sides of its control room. I'll work out the formula for a transparent metal right away."

"Right," Carson said rather dazedly "I'll— I'll see to it."

* * * * * * *

Acting under the advice of the scientists, the American Congress deliberately treated the ultimatum of the Unknown—for such Van Rutter was to all save the Association—with contempt. The same line was adopted by every other country, but behind the scenes every nation carefully marshaled its armaments just in case. Even had the scientists not advised ignoring the warning, there would have been no concession to the Unknown anyway. The world was too well supplied with military equipment to give way before threats.

What Van Rutter and Elford thought of the defiance was not known, and certainly nobody was much concerned anyway. Clever propaganda had convinced the masses of every nation that the French affair had been a natural disaster, on which a European power— it did not say which—had cashed in, in an audacious effort to get world control. Every nation disowned the unknown planes, Russia included. The whole thing was a trick. It was marvelous how the propaganda experts sweated blood to clear the air.

But in the laboratories of the American Science Association, Dake Bradfield worked with unceasing effort, had the entire staff working day and night in shifts to help him. He seemed tireless, heedless of sleep, his mind always superhumanly keen, and his manner still retaining that hint of mystery that had been present with him ever since his return. To Sheila he was a complete paradox. That passionate love he had had for her before seemed to have vanished; instead, she had become absorbed in the small army of workers he relentlessly directed.

Nobody had the remotest understanding of the scientific principles involved in the work they performed. They only knew that, in order, they created a metal as transparent as glass and tougher than tungsten, which was promptly molded to shape and replaced the ordinary metal body of a roomy, high-powered plane; that they rebuilt a radio transmitter-receiver to embody atomic force, which was put in the plane's control room; that the plane's engines were converted to use the power of tanks of water.

Then lastly they went to work on a device like a searchlight, fitted on universal bearings, its internal workings small but compact, utterly complex except to Dake's agile brain, containing all the necessary self-contained power to produce atomic force which afterwards passed through the mesh of apparatus for transforming it to the particular wavelength Dake would require. The thing was a miracle of engineering and scientific genius.

On the evening of the third day the projector was finished, and mounted inside the airplane's transparent control room. The idea of the transparence immediately became evident to the others. By this means the projector could swing freely in any direction and pass its powers through the glasslike metal without disrupting it in the process.

But Dake was not satisfied even then. In between times he had been engaged on remodeling an ordinary compass. Now it stood among the equipment— an almost airless glass globe in the center of which was a needle, the whole being sunk in a mercury bath to ensure a perpendicular position no matter how the plane rolled. Evidently it suited Dake, for he smiled grimly as he nodded to it.

"The first atomic force detector in the world," he murmured.

"You mean it will even detect atomic force from the air?" asked Carson in surprise.

"Its range is thirty thousand feet in any direction, and we shan't get that high up. I'll find Van Rutter as sure as if he signaled his presence."

Dake turned away, looked round on Sheila, Carson, and Jerry the pilot, seated at the control board.

"Guess we're all set," Dake said briefly, giving the door a final twist on the screws. "Sure you know how to handle this atomic power properly, Jerry?"

"A cinch," the burly aeronaut retorted. "With this new streamlining outside, we'll reach supersonic speed with ease."

"O.K., let's get started. First, the Brant Building!"

CHAPTER 5
UNIVERSAL ENERGY

Within a few minutes the plane was sweeping over the vast, evening lit mass of the metropolis. The city lay below in all its compact huddle of mighty edifices, most of them already streaming with lights and night sky signs. The sunset reflected pale pink in the waters round Manhattan Island.

Gaining altitude at length, the machine turned eastward, and made a beeline for the rearing mammoth of steel and masonry that was the Brant Building.

"Notice!" Dake said suddenly, as they came nearer, and he jerked his head towards the compass. The needle had steadied and was pointing directly at the building.

"We know that there must be some play of atomic forces going on in those buried laboratories there," Dake resumed. "Even if we did not know, you see how infallibly the compass reveals it. The moment the needle is dead vertical, we know that atomic force lies right below us. That's going to be useful for Van Rutter. First, though, we have this to attend to."

He turned and gripped the handles of his queer projector, swung it round until the sights were on the massive edifice with its multitude of lighted windows. It swept nearer—then Sheila gave a sudden exclamation as she stared through the transparent floor beneath her feet.

"Dake, what exactly are you going to do?"

"Reduce that building to primal space, blast a hole

a mile deep under its foundations. There will be a free emptiness and air, with the buildings on either side untouched. I can measure this power to a hair's breadth—"

"But Dake...." The girl turned and seized his arm. "Dake, do you realize there are hundreds of employees in that building? You can't destroy them too! They are innocent—"

Dake's face set implacably. "If I don't destroy them and the building, I don't destroy Elford and the laboratories. I leave a source of deadly munitions untouched. In the end thousands, even millions, will die instead of the few hundred in that edifice. Out of the way, Sheila, please!"

She looked her horror even though she obeyed. The streak of ruthlessness in Dake's nature secretly appalled her. She looked below her again, for a moment caught something of the tenseness of the situation, as the giant building became the sole focal point through the floor. The street in front of it yawned like a light-dotted chasm. Sheila clutched her father to steady herself.

"Now!" breathed Dake suddenly.

He closed the power switches. The effect of the projector's strange vibration was not immediately evident.

From top to bottom the Brant Building became insubstantial, like the illusion of a dream world. It hung transparent, incredibly for a moment with the figures of people momentarily visible through the suddenly glassified walls—then with staggering abruptness the whole 1,000-foot mass snapped into black extinction! Its very foundations changed to cavernous darkness. Where there had been the Brant Building, there was nothing but an abysmal crater, sheerly cut. A yawning emptiness divided the two buildings on each side, both of them quite untouched.

"Stupendous!" whispered Carson. "No disturbance. Not a sound."

"Instant straightening of space warp, not a resolution of matter into energy," Dake said quietly. "That is why there is no noise."

"And hundreds, perhaps thousands, of lives wiped out," Sheila muttered. "People who had their lives to live, who had other people depending on them."

But her secret hope that Dake would show compassion was not realized. Instead he said gravely, "Hundreds against millions," and patted the projector lovingly. Then he glanced at Jerry.

"Head toward Russia!"

Sheila stood looking back at that yawning hole amidst the other buildings. Deep, unplumbed thoughts stirred through her mind.

* * * * * * *

It was midnight, after a seeming eternity of flying, before the compass reacted over a vast, deserted stretch of land on the western frontiers of Russia. In silence the party stared down on bleak, unlighted darkness stretching as far as their view could encompass.

"Down there," Dake said slowly, "is Van Rutter's

hidden retreat, obviously underground. Planes and atomic force that he thought he could conceal, eh?"

He smiled twistedly, watched the compass needle tensely as it swung slowly to the vertical. Gently he turned the projector's nose downward. Then he slammed home the switches.

It was impossible to see what happened but moments later the blaze of searchlights revealed a landscape riven like the Grand Canyon, the sides of the chasm sheer and smooth. From the remote depths came a steamy bubbling of inner discharges. Whatever had lain there, whatever vast enterprise Van Rutter had controlled, had gone forever. Without a sound or light, extinction had caught up with him.

Dake laughed slightly, a hard bitter laugh that made the others in the control room glance at one another.

"Never before did I realize how sweet a thing vengeance can be," Dake muttered, serious again. "They showed me no mercy, and I in return showed them none."

"Well, the threat of war is destroyed anyway," Carson said thankfully. "What comes next?"

Dake glanced at him. "I shall make war instead."

"What!"

"Not exactly in the way you think. You'll see what I am aiming at before long. First, I have a radio broadcast to transmit to the world, hence our high-powered instrument."

Dake switched on the atomic force-driven transmitter and waited a moment as the power surged through it.

"Enough power to swamp every other broadcast in existence," he commented in satisfaction. "Just as Van Rutter did. And since for all practical purposes I am going to broadcast from the approximate spot he used, I shall *be* him, with a change of plan."

Carson and Sheila said nothing, but like Jerry at the controls they frowned in some mystification as Dake pulled the microphone to him and spoke in a passable imitation of Van Rutter's voice.

"Governments of the world! Your ultimatum would have expired at midnight tomorrow night. But due to your continued silence I have decided on certain amendments, and I have given yet another proof of my powers by destroying the Brant Building in New York more completely than anything was ever destroyed before. Again I say I do not want actual bloodshed. But I shall cripple your power to attack me! Your secret armament factories, your hidden zones of destruction, will avail you nothing. Your one alternative to save yourselves from me is to destroy your weapons of war voluntarily and relinquish control to me. I shall expect a radio response within thirty minutes. If you refuse, then prepare for the worse! If you accept, I will advise you further. That is all."

Dake switched off, stood reflecting.

"Just what is the idea?" Carson demanded. "Seems to me you might as well have let Van Rutter get on with the job! You're just as bad!"

"You do me an injustice," Dake said quietly. "Van

Rutter intended to launch a ruthless massacre against the peoples of the world in the hope of frightening the rest of them into submission, over which, with the help of atomic power, he could have become self-appointed king. I have no such ideas."

"Then why imitate Van Rutter?"

"Because the blame for what is going to happen may as well be laid at the door of the man whom people call the Unknown, otherwise Van Rutter. He had already made himself the target, so people may as well go on thinking they're shooting at him." Dake stopped and then asked a surprising question. "In the old days, what did one do to get a fox out of his lair when all else had failed?"

"Smoke him out, I guess," said Sheila. "So what?"

"Humanity collectively is the fox this time, which I am smoking out. How else can one find out where different nations' armament centers are without actual recourse to threat of war? Think of the countless secret hiding places which only possible war can reveal. The expectation of attack will make every nation tear down its camouflage. But for the advent of Van Rutter, humanity would have thrown itself at each other in time in any case, from sheer necessity of economic pressure and the need to *use* the vast weight of arms before they became white elephants. The arms would *have* to be used in order to get the money from another country—if beaten in war—to pay for them. One vast, vicious circle strangling progress which only a strong man with infinite power can break down. I am that man!"

"Go on," Carson was listening attentively.

"Well, don't you see that Van Rutter changed the situation? Instead of nations preparing to hurl themselves at each other, they would have banded together against him. And, had he lived, he would have triumphed because of superior power. But if we still let the world believe he is in action, we can draw them into the open, let them waste their activities on us—for they can't possibly harm us—and at the same time we will destroy their arms without actually injuring anybody, beyond those few we cannot avoid. In other words, we'll draw the fangs and roots of war right out of the planet!"

"Destroy armaments forever, tear down the barriers to reason and progress," Sheila whispered. "Oh Dake dearest, that's wonderful— But just why do you keep up the pretense of Van Rutter? Why not reveal that—"

"Do you think any nation would feel kindly toward a power bent on destroying its arms, even if it knew it *was* the Science Association? No, Sheila—definitely no! We don't intend any harm, but we cannot make anybody believe that. It is better that fury be directed at a now extinct Van Rutter while the Science Association remains unsuspected. Of course, my ultimatum will be refused. I only gave it at all to keep up the illusion. Strange, but Van Rutter did far more for the peace of the future world than he ever intended."

"And afterward?" Carson glanced up morosely. "More arms, more build up, more conflict. It will take even more than you to destroy warlike notions in the minds of men, Dake."

Dake smiled, that same superior smile that seemed to make him like a god. "I have the knowledge of the dead, Doc, and with that so many, many things are possible." He pondered. "It all depends on whether I have the time," he ended slowly.

That oft repeated ambiguity was not questioned this time. Dake stood looking at the radio receiver, waiting. And his judgment was correct. Before the thirty minutes had expired the first answer came through.

Refusal! America would fight to the death! So would Great Britain, all Europe, the East....

Dake smiled. "O.K., Jerry. Home!"

* * * * * * *

Once more in the safety of the Association's laboratories, there was not a little grim amusement among the inmates, all of them in the know, as they watched the preparations of the world for battle with a still unknown and merciless attacker. The rumble of defensive movements spread across the Earth in all directions. America too, mobilized all her forces. All unaware of the trick, the President called on the Science Association for assistance in this time of grave crisis. Carson gravely promised to do all he could.

Dake waited for a week, surveying through television and news reports the revelation of different nations' armament centers and fortresses. For his own part in between times, he had a new plant installed in the plane which, using atomic force as usual, surrounded the flyer with an impenetrable shell of energy. The plane was black, resembling those of the Van Rutter fleet. The glass center, though transparent from within, was opaque from outside.

Beyond loading the plane up with ample provisions, there was nothing more to be done. Dake gave the world four days to bring its toys into view, then as before, with Sheila, Carson, and Jerry he entered the plane at ten in the morning of October 29, 1980.

When Teny had forced the plane to a considerable height, Dake stood looking down on New York far below, surveying the centers of defense that had been contrived for the safety of the civilian population. He smiled, lowered the projector downward, sighted it on an antiaircraft unit near Times Square. He closed the switches.

That action was the spark that lighted the whole powder magazine. The swift, resistless changing of the Times Square unit into a bottomless pit started the American air fleet on the warpath. From north, south, east, and west they came in their droning, vengeful hundreds to do battle with this audacious individual who fancied he could rule the world.

Dake took no notice of them! He did not attack them. They either smashed their planes in pieces against the defensive energy shell, or else, baffled by the mysterious powers of their adversary, turned tail with a view to conference with the higher-ups before going any further.

And Dake went on with his task calmly and steadily, flying at three thousand feet, tearing every armament and defensive dump out of the earth as be came over it, destroying people too where the margin was too fine for his selective instruments to avoid them.

In between the attacks he radioed warnings to the battle fleet gathered round the coast of the Americas. Either evacuate the ships within an hour, or be destroyed with them! Commanders hesitated, glanced up at that black speck in the blue, and wondered. They knew already they were tackling an invincible foe, yet one with a curious streak of mercy. They decided to evacuate.

Sure enough, within the hour the black speck returned. One by, one, completely and mysteriously, thousands of millions of dollars' worth of steel and defensive equipment vanished from the water. The men in the little bobbing boats watched in dazed amazement, clung tightly to their seats as tumbling water came surging toward them. But they were unhurt.

* * * * * * *

Throughout the day Dake went on steadily, flying back and forth with stupendous speed across the continent, constantly shattering everything of a warlike nature he came across. Time and again fleets of bombers harried him futilely. Their bombs bounced away harmlessly: some of the planes were sent crashing to earth or disappeared in mid air. This soundless primal power, the sudden straightening out of etheric folds, was something no man could tackle.

It was evening by the time they left American shores—left it a continent without a weapon, a continent filled with baffled millions who could not believe that the Unknown was content to leave them thus, disarmed but unhurt.

So Dake went on, on the most incredible conquest in history.

For a week the airplane never touched ground, darting back and forth across the Earth, untouched by man's most demoniacal powers. And one by one, in every country, weapons and arms centers and potential battlefields and fleets were transformed into emptiness. Ships sank, planes disappeared. Not a country escaped Dake's ruthless tooth-combing. In one week he swept the earth clean of every destructive device man had ever owned or known.

Only then, content that he had not destroyed a single life willingly, did he return unseen to New York under the shadow of night, went back to the Association laboratory. His first act was to get the radio-transmitters to work, cutting out the flow of world news—a world still dazed with wonder and still desperately afraid.

"Peoples of the world!" Dake said quietly into the microphone. "Get your interpreters to work so all may understand me. People, you have been tricked for your own good! I forced you into the open with your popguns and pistols in order that I could destroy them. Realize one thing—The man who would have dominated you and performed inhuman massacre for his own ends, is dead. I killed him with an infinitely great power. Who I am does not matter: I have already proved to you I do not wish to harm anybody.

"But I *do* intend to bring to this world a peace it has lacked since the world began! I can do it because I know things no man ever knew before. You cannot stop me, not even the most warlike of you. *Nobody* can stop me! But I give you warning here—I am going to give certain orders to the ruling heads of each country, and those orders must be followed to the absolute letter. If they are not, I shall know of it and I shall destroy without hesitation. I will only be merciful if you obey. But your obedience is not because I intend to dominate you, but because it is to your eventual advantage that you should obey. This is not an ultimatum: a man with infinite power makes no ultimatums. Now listen attentively.

"Marshal together your finest engineers and scientists: you will have two days in which to do this. At the end of that time your engineers will take down the instructions I shall give. In each country of importance there will be installed a vast atomic power generating station. It is a power that can advance civilization two hundred years and more. One man tried to abuse it: none other will ever do that again! You have your orders for now. Obey them or take the consequences—and if any man dares to try and create a warlike weapon in the interval, I shall know of it and destroy him!"

Because nations could do nothing else, and also because most of the responsible heads believed in the

Unknown's honest intentions—Dake's orders were followed to the letter. There was surprise, even bewilderment, but the thing was done.

The moment it was, Dake, watching every move with anxious diligence, started a fresh radio broadcast, this time with complicated instructions comprehensible only to the engineers, and not always to them. But at least they knew what to do even if they did not entirely know why they did it. They were like men mastering the uses of electricity without knowing what electricity is.

The broadcasts followed at regular intervals when, through television, Dake was assured the work had progressed as far as he had ordered. Simultaneously, through the weeks, there grew up in America, Great Britain, Europe, and the Orient, enormous structures of specially cast metal, with adjacent power houses fixed in uniform formation nearby, from which led power feeds to the different nerve centers of various nearby cities.

The powerhouses themselves made their very builders gasp in stunned admiration. They could not even guess at the uncanny genius of the being who had devised all this from abstract thinking. But it was perfectly clear to them that here in these mighty power plants, from the mere breakdown of water into its atomic energy, was unlimited power for the development of commerce, railways, air-service, and all the amenities of civilized life.

But what would the price be? It was inconceivable

that a man should give the world such power without demanding a heavy reward. World dictatorship, perhaps?

When Dake heard of this, he only smiled. But his smile was not enough for Dr. Carson and Sheila. They wanted to know why, particularly Sheila. But when she came to look for him in the Association laboratories one morning, he had disappeared, and nobody seemed to know what had become of him. Nor did Dr. Carson seem to deem it wise to investigate too thoroughly in case it happened to be against Dake's wishes. He would probably return when he was ready.

To Sheila it was an impossible situation. There were still many things she did not understand—or her father either for that matter. But all her searching drew a blank—then ten days after Dake had vanished, she got a phone call from him.

Would she come to the address he gave, and promise to tell nobody until afterward? She gave her immediate assent, puzzling over the place he named: it mentioned a little spot some five miles from Monterey in California. He would meet her, disguised, at the San Francisco airport.

He did, disguised in dark glasses and sticking plaster as on that first occasion. From the airport he drove in a closed sedan along the Pacific coastline road, passed through Monterey itself, finally stopped at a small, isolated little house on a steep shelf of land sweeping down to the open, sunlit sea.

Only when he had garaged the car and was in the

house did he seem ready to talk.

"I had to send for you," he said, in a low voice.

"But Dake, why did you have to go like that?" the girl asked earnestly. "Do you not realize that you are a public figure? The greatest benefactor the world has ever known?"

"I know." He stared through the open French doors toward the sea. "That was one reason why I left when my work was done. If any credit is going about, let your father have it, Sheila. I can never have it. I am legally dead."

"But you came back to life!" she insisted. "We can marry now, do all we planned, live in this wonderfully happy world of your creating—"

"No!" His voice was stonily firm. He looked steadily at her flushed, eager young face. "That can never be, my dear," he went on, with a vague semblance of his old tenderness. "God knows, I would that it could, but—I'm only a ghost, a ghost who must die again. Soon."

Sheila paled. "Dake, you don't mean—"

He fell silent, staring out to sea.

"I had the time while in the laboratories to examine the instruments Doc lowered down the mine shaft," he went on presently. "I know now what happened. When that atomic shell dropped to earth, it released its energy. That energy mingled with slight radium deposits in pitchblende, which were certainly around that spot. The combination of the two energies produced a form of mitogenesis, the basic radiation of life. Anyhow, enormously powerful waves of mitogenetic radiation were given off. They affected my dead heart like a charge of super-adrenalin. I recovered. My organs were in order: I had died only through insufficient oxygen. I had fallen slackly into mud and was unhurt. So I came back to life. To Mason those radiations brought death. His heart accelerated far beyond normal and he couldn't take it."

"So that was it," Sheila whispered.

Dake gave a bitter smile. "As I have suspected all along, there is a price. The life-return is not permanent! It is only a superficial thing that burns itself out. All along I have been desperately afraid I would not finish in time. I dare not love you again, my dear, knowing I must die!"

The girl did not speak. Her eyes were chained to him as he sat slumped in the chair by the window.

"The fires of this spurious life are burning low. I have only a few hours left. I know it now. I came here intending to die without anybody ever knowing—but I had to see you again, explain the true facts. I chose this spot where I could gaze out over the beauty of a world I must leave, dragging out a few more hours of happiness given to me by an accident of nature."

He got to his feet suddenly, put an arm around the girl's shoulders.

"Sheila, I found atomic force," he murmured. "It killed me: it gave me life back again: it gave me greater knowledge than man has ever known: it enabled me to give peace to my fellow beings: it showed me beyond death, and now...it is over."

"It hasn't *got* to be!" she shouted frantically. "Dake, you belong to me, to the world— It isn't right that this should be your reward."

He was silent, chin on chest.

"You must find a way!" she whispered, clasping his arm.

He still pondered, then said quietly, "Give me ten minutes, Sheila, to make a last experiment. It would be too harrowing for you to witness. I believe there is a last chance! Come in here."

He threw open an adjoining door, and she passed into a small, sunlit study. She crossed to the armchair moodily and sank down into it, wondering what possible scheme Dake could have in mind. In desperate impatience she waited, tried the door once and found it locked. Not a sound reached her.

At the end of the ten minutes she tried the door again. To her surprise it opened instantly. Immediately her gaze went to the open French doors, the cool wind from the sea blowing back the curtains. Automatically her eyes were caught by a sheet of white notepaper held down with the paperweight. Mechanically she picked it up, read through a blur of tears.

"Dearest: There never was a way! Forgive my deception, but I had to make it as easy as possible for you. All my notes, except the for-mula for atomic force, which I have destroyed, together with a full account of events to date,

are m my bureau in the study. Give them to Dr. Carson.

"I prefer it this way. It is better than waiting for the inevitable end. If my body is ever found it will not matter, because no man ever knew what happened to Dake Bradfield, except our own intimate friends.

"Remember me always, my dearest.

"Dake."

Mechanically Sheila blundered to the window, the wind fanning her hot, tear-scalded cheeks.

"Dake!" she screamed. "Dake—!"

The empty stretch of beach only gave back the echo of her voice. Words died in her throat. Her eyes were following a man's footprints going down from the windows, across the sand to where the Pacific rollers creamed and foamed in the sunshine.

There was nothing alive in sight, only the lonely, circling gulls.

MARK GRAYSON
UNLIMITED

As the closest friend of the late Dr. Mark Grayson, I feel that I am called upon to relate the full details of his amazing experiment. I cannot stand idly by and hear him referred to as a lunatic who finally made a mysterious exit from his prison cell, because I knew him to be one of the most brilliant, though maybe misguided, scientists of our time.

From early college days when we had used to room together he had always been interested in interatomic physics, with particular leanings towards Schrödinger, and Heisenberg with his Principle of Indeterminacy. What exactly he gleaned from the treatises and theories of these two great scientific thinkers I did not discover until later years—and then I did it with a vengeance!

After college was over, our ways perforce parted, and I heard nothing of Mark for many years. I married, and settled down to quite a thriving practice as attorney in New York. Then one day I found that he was in the news—and none too pleasantly either. Apparently he had been ridiculed by the Association of Science for setting forth some new theory connected with the electron. In the report I read of the meeting it was pretty clear that Mark had had the worst of it and as a gesture of protest had resigned his position as Professor of Interatomic Physics to the Association.

Just about like old Mark! Ridicule was the one thing he had never been able to stand, and evidently he had not altered his views much in the passing years. Hearing about him, though, brought old memories back to me, and so I wrote him a letter, asking the newspaper to forward it to him. I made a point of sympathizing with him, but I also admitted that owing to my limited scientific knowledge, I had no idea whether he had been right or wrong. Back came his answer very shortly—his address showed he was living now on Long Island—and it was typical of him:

My dear Arthur—

It was a delight to hear from you again, and even better to have your sympathy. I do not need it, though. It should be given to those dolts in the Association. I verily believe they do not know the difference between an electron and a piece of cheese! Why don't you come over to my place for a few days and renew the friendship? Maybe I can explain to you how monumental a thing it is to be able to detect an electron for the first time in scientific history.

Always yours sincerely,

Mark Grayson

When I showed the wife the letter she decided to pay a visit to her sister, and it being a fairly quiet period in the city, I took time out and went over to Long Island to see what exactly Mark was getting at.

Obviously he had made plenty of money, anyhow. His home was a truly beautiful place, and adequately staffed by a very immobile manservant and an even more immobile housekeeper. I found later that they were husband and wife, and deaf-mutes. Evidently Mark was taking no chances on his secrets travelling elsewhere. Mark himself was well enough. He was three years my senior, but work and worry had made him look a good deal more than that. His wild, disorderly hair was streaked prematurely with gray, his small, energetic form was even thinner than when he had been a youth—but there was no doubt that the creative fires of energy still burned within him. He moved and talked swiftly. His quick blue eyes darted inquiry and challenge alternately. He was what the novelists would call a restless, highly intellectual soul, with no time for trifles and even less for derision.

I arrived in mid-afternoon, and until eight in the evening we exchanged notes of the passed years and recalled the happy things we had done. No word about science escaped his lips. He had remained a bachelor, I think, because his work had kept him too preoccupied to admit of him even looking at a woman, let alone marrying one.

Then, suddenly, without any inducement on my part, he came to the matter I was wondering about. It was after dinner, when he sat chewing a short cigar.

"What do you know about the electron, Arthur?" he asked me, standing with his back to the library fire. "You are an attorney and an intelligent man. I ask you because I don't want to waste time explaining something you may know already."

"Always in a hurry, aren't you?" I smiled. "Well, all I know about an electron is that it is—I think—the smallest particle of electricity."

"The deplorable uselessness of education!" he groaned, raising his hands deprecatingly. "Obviously I shall have to start from the beginning if you are ever to understand what I am getting at. Just come along with me, Arthur, and I'll open your eyes."

Rather amused at his general air of impatience, I followed him out of the room to his private laboratory, and then stood for a moment or two looking round on instruments and apparatus I could never hope to understand. He perched himself on a stool, and now he was amidst these weird creations of his genius, he looked really at home.

"An electron has so far only been a theory—or better still a probability," he said, his eyes fixed on me.

I squatted down on an empty crate opposite him.

"One of the big stumbling blocks to scientific progress has been the inability of man to say that the electron is either here or there," he went on. "Until I studied the problem we knew that the electron, while obeying the mathematical laws of waves and ripples, was also a particle. But it could not be placed. It existed somewhere within a wave group, but that wave group was indefinite in extent. It had no sharp limitation. It just trailed off into surrounding space, even into other dimensions. For all we knew it might extend into infinity. So far all we have known is that the electron exists, but that its exact position is purely a probability in the equation of waves."

"You're going pretty deep, Mark," I said, pondering. "But go on—I'll try and follow you."

"You recall that I used to study Heisenberg a lot? He outlined the Principle of Indeterminacy—that it is impossible to know both the position and velocity of an electron at a chosen moment. Measure one and the other changes immediately. Since both factors are necessary to an absolute deduction, it looked as if Man would never be able to metaphorically put his finger on the electron's position. Of course, approximate deductions could be made by the very reason of the electron's area of waves being so inconceivably small. But science does not like things to approximate, Arthur. It demands incontestable fact."

Mark paused for a moment, drawing at his cigar. Then he gave a rather cynical grin.

"I found out how to extend the area of an electron wave," he commented. "Instead of allowing the waves to be infinitesimal and shading off into space or other dimensions, I devised electrical equipment reacting directly on the subatomic waves of matter. The result is that I can extend the wave area of an electron indefinitely, and more than that! The strain produced by extending these waves produces a definite reaction in one exact part of the extended wave. In that exact part we find—the electron! I believe, had I decided to finish the subatomic microscope I had in mind, it would have been possible to view the electron as one would a planet through a telescope. But I am not going on with that idea—not now."

A hard note had crept into his voice—and I glanced at him in surprise.

"But why not?" I exclaimed. "It would surely be the greatest achievement of your career?"

"You remember how I was treated by the Association?" he asked bitterly. "Their attitude is why I have called an end to my experiment. The Association was of the opinion that my discovery was absurd—that years of experiment had served to turn my head! Far from them agreeing to look into my findings, or perhaps helping me to finish off the finer details of the discovery, they laughed at me to scorn. Prejudice still exists, Arthur, even in these days. For that very reason I am going to have my revenge on them—on everybody on this whole stupid planet! You can't laugh at science and get away with it."

The change in his manner rather startled me for a moment. I had always known him to be a pretty erratic sort of fellow, with perhaps a good share of that curious vindictiveness that sometimes goes alongside great genius, but here something ugly was cropping up. It was in every line of his bearing.

"What more details could be needed to such an experiment?" I asked quietly, trying to keep him on the straight track.

"Plenty! I was handicapped at the Association because I was not able to give a concrete demonstration of my theory. To have done that would have produced unpredictable results. You see, Arthur, this extension of electronic wavelength automatically crushes—or at least telescopes—the wavelengths of the electrons immediately surrounding them, and the effect would be progressive. It would be rather like a railway siding. You have seen how a truck is shunted, and how perhaps a hundred trucks all jolt after the first one has been shoved by the locomotive? That is the same effect in principle.

"To extend one area will mean a progressive jolting of electronic waves in all directions from the source of the disturbance. Now, an electron wave has a range that may pass into infinity—which means, into the greater macrocosm of our universe. It also operates, as Schrödinger told us, in three dimensions. But two electrons operate in six dimensions, three in nine, and so forth, Can you for a moment grasp the bewildering complexity of one electron with its wavelength held out in indefinite stress for maximum distance? An area would be disturbed all around it, and the very structure of space and matter would be shifted!"

"In that case," I said, looking at him fixedly and

thinking hard, "it might mean the end of the world!"

"It would," he said, grinning. "Or at least it would, if I know my scientific facts. What's needed is a careful experiment to render such a possibility impossible. I have not enlarged an electron wave yet, but I know I could do it. It might take me many years to find a way of isolating this freak wave to prevent a wholesale disturbance, but for this the Association is not prepared to wait. They wanted results immediately. Because I had to refrain from giving them, I—well, I walked out."

"Then you are going to complete the problem on your own?" I asked.

He stubbed out his cigar, and got off the stool. Coming over to me he regarded me steadily.

"No. I am not!" His voice was deadly quiet. "I realise that if science in this day and age cannot credit the word of one of its most famous members, it is time that such science and the devotees of it be destroyed! I am going to extend the area of an electron wave and consequences be hanged!"

I got up quickly and caught at his arm.

"But you just said it would be dangerous!" I protested.

"That it would, perhaps, destroy the world?" he went on. "Yes, that's exactly what I believe it will do. But don't you see, it will have proved that I am right. I'll have proved I can extend the wave of an electron. If it does not destroy the world, it will mean that the area is there ready to view once a subatomic microscope is prepared. I shall have provided the proof. If it does destroy the world—well, I'd sooner lose a mighty discovery and my own life in a cataclysm than have a lot of fools grinning at me!"

"Look here, Mark, you can't do this!" I said firmly, holding on to him. "You are only looking at it from your own viewpoint. You are bitter and vindictive, like you used to be at school when old Haldane said you dreamed too much. I steered you right then, and I'm going to now. You can't do this thing!"

Mark stared at me a moment. His face hardened, became ruthless.

"I can—and I'm going to," he answered steadily. "I asked you to come here so that you can be a witness to my actions. I shall need proof if my experiment is successful and the world still stays in place afterwards.... I'm not mad, you know," he added seriously.

No, he was not mad—not in the accepted sense, anyway. But he was consumed with mortified rage that anybody should dare to question his genius. Amazing though it was, it seemed I had on my hands the unenviable job of trying to save a whole universe from his too clever hands.

I released him and stood trying to think things out, my mind running round the idea of physical violence. He left me and walked across to a complicated switchboard controlling many massive and unfamiliar instruments.

"This is my electron-wave extender," he said. "It reacts on the subatomic waves The energy it generates strikes into the densest part of the electron waves. By this means they do not shade off into infinity, but are built up in intensity until they have the same strength as the source. Since electrons are everywhere, be it matter or space, it simply does not signify where I apply the energy. But for the sake of accuracy, it might as well be a fixed point."

He turned aside and picked up a small sealed ampoule. It looked to be empty. Gently he set it down on the big circular plate immediately within the range of his queerly fashioned projectors.

"This ampoule is filled with hydrogen gas," he explained. If you remember your physics you will recall that it is the least dense substance in our material Periodic Table, and therefore the easiest one to deal with in the search for an electron—granting there ever is a search later on."

He began to fiddle with switches and controls, and all of a sudden it occurred to me what he was planning to do while I simply stood and watched. I acted instantly! Lunging at him, I caught his arm just as he threw the master switch. He staggered backwards and fell, half sprawling, across the flat metal plate where he had laid his ampoule of hydrogen. For a second or two he just lay there, dazed, then I hauled him up again, pushed him into a chair, and snapped off the master switch I had seen him operate.

"You are not going to do this thing," I declared grimly. "Not even if I have to beat the daylights out of you to make you see reason. Later on you'll thank me, too."

He sat there looking at me, glowering in fact—then

gradually the light died out of his eyes and he got to his feet.

"I wonder if you realize something?" he said slowly. "I fell on that plate right in the area of that energy of mine! It hit me—all over! What I had intended for the hydrogen sample reacted on me instead. I wonder what will happen?" he finished, pondering.

"Nothing," I assured him. "You weren't under the influence long enough for anything to happen."

He did not say anything for a moment, then he gave a little shrug.

"Just chance that it happened that way," he shrugged. "It might prove to be interesting later on."

I could plainly see that whatever danger there might be did not distress him in the least. He was true scientist enough to be always interested in the unusual, even if he was the victim.

"Let's get back to the library," I urged him. "You need to rest up a bit. Too much work and too much ridicule haven't done you any good, you know."

He smiled and then nodded, but though he said nothing, I could tell that some deep thought or other was back of his mind....

* * * * * * *

The following day, much to my annoyance, I received an urgent telephone call from home requesting my presence at the office right away for an important legal case—so, just as I had been getting interested, I was forced to take my leave of Mark and plunge forthwith into the intricacies of a criminal action.

He parted from me cordially enough, but I noticed an enigmatic smile about his lips as he shook hands. It was the smile of a man who knows something tremendous and won't speak about it. Then, back in New York, with all the curriculum of legal work around me. I soon forgot all about Mark and his amazing doings.

For a week anyway—then one evening I was working late in my office when I saw somebody standing before me at the desk. For a second or two I questioned the credibility of it, because I had locked the door to ensure privacy and the window was thirty-five stories up. Yet there he was—Mark Grayson, smiling cynically, his hair disordered, and his body having a curiously transparent quality.

"Mark!" I exclaimed, astounded, getting up and stretching out my hand in greeting. "How are you? How did you get in?"

Then, in a flash he was gone! I blinked, rubbed my eyes, then went over to the switch and put the lights on. So far I had only had the desk lamp in action. He had disappeared, all right.

I was not exactly frightened, just puzzled. I am not a believer in ghosts, but I do think there is something to premonition and pre-vision. Suppose he had died at the self-same moment and that I had had a pre-death visitation? Immediately I reached for the telephone. His voice answered me promptly enough.

"You saw me?" he repeated, as I explained matters. "Well, maybe you need your eyes tested. Or else...." He stopped and I guessed he was thinking hard. "Sort of transparent?" he asked pensively.

"Seemed so—like a fairly solid ghost; I could just see the wall through you—or it, or whatever it was."

"Mighty interesting, because at the exact time you've mentioned I was thinking about you," he said. "I must study this over carefully. It may be the first reaction of that accidental fall I had into the midst of that energy machine of mine."

"You are feeling well?" I asked anxiously.

"Never better. And I'm not going to destroy the world, so don't you worry. Your commonsense lecture did me good. I mean to find a way to produce electronic isolation. See you again."

I rang off, sat thinking for a moment or two, then shrugged my shoulders. If there was a scientific explanation for it, I certainly did not know what it was....

As it transpired, though, this was only the beginning. Two more days went by, then the newspapers published a full column on Mark Grayson. When I read it I found it had been culled from the experiences of quite a lot of different people in widely separated parts of the country. Each person interviewed reported having seen a vaguely transparent figure resembling Mark Grayson. Sometimes he had been observed within five minutes, in places as much as two hundred miles apart. Some witnesses, though perhaps they were drawing on their imaginations, declared that he had merged into two and even three persons, all identical. This had happened while the witnesses were watching him.

To me, especially, it was puzzling, and I wished my legal work over so that I could pay him another visit. The first moment I was free, I hurried to Long Island and found him, apparently not disturbed, though he did not look as well as he had on my earlier trip.

"Glad you've come," he said, in that offhand way he had, when we were in his laboratory. "These happenings are rather alarming if you don't understand them. As it happens I do, partly. You know, I've been having the devil of a time with newspaper men. They have been here pestering me. It appears that I am rapidly becoming a public nuisance. All I can do is deny everything, and that does not improve my case very much. If I am not careful, I'm likely to find myself in an ugly mess."

"But how in the world do you account for these appearances of yourself in so many widely differing places?" I demanded. "You could never have been to such places. Time and distance would not permit it!"

"I think I have unlocked a door of science which I never intended to touch," he said, thinking. "And it may mean the end of me. It's likely the extension of an electronic wavelength reacts differently in living organism to what it does in inert matter. A piece of iron, for instance, would transmit disturbance to all surrounding matter and bring about a general cataclysm, but organic, or living matter, is different. The effect is transmitted through that body until it is dissipated!

"Mind force enters into it, too. Living matter is at the behest of the mind, as we know, but so far only the living body itself has responded to the mind. In my case it is different. By accidentally falling into the area of that energy transmission, I enlarged the wavelength of a whole mass of my electrons indefinitely, displaced the energy thereof, if you will. The result is that confusion has entered into my matter makeup. The displacement of the wavelengths has produced an emission of energy, and each time the energy passes away it has to resolve itself. That is electronic law. The resolution takes the form of a complete image of me, a thin, attenuated image, which travels immediately to the spot I happen to be thinking of at the time, or somewhere in the immediate vicinity. Mind is at the back of it all the time because mind is at the back of the parent body.

"But there is a price for it, Arthur. With each emission of energy, as more electrons extend their wavelengths and pass away from my physical makeup, I lose substance and weight. Mind I cannot lose, because that is an eternal quality."

I was bewildered by what he had told me. "I don't half grasp all this," I said. "Where is it going to end?"

"I don't know," he muttered. "I believe it has only just begun. A series of thinly spaced electron setups part from me at intervals and become ghosts of Mark Grayson. There are tens of thousands of Mark Graysons remaining in my makeup yet. As I told you, one electron takes three dimensions; two, six; three, nine—and so on progressively. In time I imagine that my images will not only be hurtling to different parts of the Earth, but into other spaces, dimensions, times, and worlds. In other words I am being radiated into infinity and multiple-infinity. Maybe it is a just judgment for the plan I had to destroy the world and perhaps the universe."

"But for me it would never have happened," I protested. "I pushed you onto that plate!"

"And by so doing you perhaps saved the world." He shrugged. "What's the difference? It happened, and I'm prepared to abide by it."

That was how the matter stood with him. There was not much I could do about it, anyway, not being a particularly good scientist. But the interest of this amazing phenomenon had gripped me so hard that I sent over a call to the wife and told her I was stopping with Grayson for a day or two as he was not very well. By this decision I entered into the most astonishing few days any man ever lived.

At intervals—intervals which increased in frequency as time passed—I actually saw this parting of electronic energy from Mark Grayson. It was rather like one of those trick shots in a movie where a dreamer gets out of himself and walks about.

Suddenly, even while talking to me, or having a meal, or seated in a chair, an image of Mark would flash out from him in a hazy glow, go right through wall, floor, or ceiling, and vanish. All he did was smile wryly, recall exactly what he had been thinking about at that moment, and sure enough the image was later reported to have been seen in that exact spot.

At first this used to happen at intervals of three hours. Then as the weird progressive change built up within him, as the energy he had absorbed extended more and more multi-thousands of electron wavelengths inside him, it happened more repeatedly, until in two more days as many as twelve images parted from him in thirty minutes. In some cases they were in triplicate. I completely lost count of how many Mark Graysons went out, but we learned plenty from the television, radio, and newspapers. Some of the reports were pathetic, some startling, and others downright ludicrous.

In a far Western state a woman dying of cancer had been praying for a vision to restore her. At that identical time some quirk of Grayson's mind had sent an image right into her bedroom, a place he had merely envisaged in thought. The woman had seen the vision and been instantly cured.

In another case a famous banker had demanded action by the police because Mark had appeared through the closed doors of a secret conference and heard all the details of a great international finance deal. In yet another instance an image had appeared in England where a high-pressure estate agent had been trying to sell a castle to a wealthy traveller. The traveller had refused to buy because there was no sign of the reputed ghost. A Mark Grayson transparency glimpsed in the aged cloisters had made that agent a richer man.

Silly, trivial things, but they give an idea of what distances the parting electrons of Mark Grayson travelled, distances no longer trammelled to the ordinary limits of an electron wavelength. Then, always the true scientist, he began to see that undisciplined journeying by his images are useless. He might as well do something with them. For, as he told me, he knew what they saw and felt by reason of the mind reaction they carried. Because of this, he gradually became less sure of himself. As the images increased to the multiples he inevitably received multiple impressions, was in some cases aware of being in half a dozen places at once.

But he was determined to make something of his doom, for that was inevitably what was coming, As he got to the place where the images were so numerous they were not confined to three dimensions, but to six, nine, twelve, and multiples of three for every electron, he went literally a-roaming, and each time he told me what he had seen and done. I can only report this as he explained it.

He passed into the sixth dimension and found it populated as freely as our own three, but by beings who were purely mathematical because of their environment. He wandered across the red sands of Mars and found a truly dead world, walked beneath the clouds of torrid Venus, wandered across sun-scorched Mercury. He had, in fact, the supreme chance of all creation, the ability to roam as an actual thought-projected image into all the places locked so far to science.

He told me of his journeyings through the hottest

suns, of his visits to the centres of blazing Sirius and Antares. Then some whim changed his course. He had all Time open to him, too, as more and more electrons swept him into the multiple dimensions demanded of them.

He walked in the Cretaceous and Carboniferous Periods, saw the beginning and end of the world, established facts of history, which I wrote down and stated vital facts of the future, which only the passage of time can prove to lesser mortals. He saw ahead of us not peace and content, but a world of struggle and dreadful turmoil until Man should really come to understand that all life, intelligence, power, and conception are mental and not physical.

Plainly, Mark Grayson, unlimited in number of images and unlimited by any mortal or material barrier, was for three brief weeks a god. Then he tired of his wanderings and the vast things he had learned. The terrific strain on his mental and physical makeup broke him down. Unutterably weary, for his bodily energy had decreased with every set of electrons to pass from it, he finally ceased his mental roaming and let the images go whither chance willed. In consequence they appeared here, there, and everywhere without direction. Sometimes in the city, sometimes in the country, sometimes for good, sometimes for ill— until the very complexity of his appearances and the secrets he supposedly learned caused big shots to add their complaints to that of banker Joseph Runthorne; and finally the police came to investigate. I was present when they arrived. I tried in vain to convince them that my friend was ill and could not be disturbed.

He was sitting in the laboratory when they arrested him—a pale, white-haired man now, lines of weariness traced on his face.

"Do you deny, Dr. Grayson, that you have been projecting images of yourself here, there, and about?" asked the officer in charge. "Do you assert you haven't been using these images for the learning of secrets and the—er—violation of personal privacy?"

Grayson smiled wanly. "I admit the first and deny the second. Not that it matters. I have seen the beginning and end of the world, the beginning and end of space."

It was a pity he said this, for it sounded crazy. It was on this ground that he was brought up for trial. I was present too, of course, as chief witness, and I employed a brother lawyer of outstanding skill to defend him. But unfortunately Mark prejudiced his chances by his technical explanations.

To me, knowing him as he had been, it was quite clear that the mass pf knowledge he had amassed and the energy he was still losing had caused him to lose his grip on his mind. He sounded—and maybe he was—crazy. Certainly the regular glowing of light about him which pronounced the departure of more images did a great deal to get him convicted as a criminal lunatic. He was removed to prison to await confinement in an institution for the criminally insane.

I was allowed to see him for a few minutes, and

found him quite rational again. I took good care to keep my distance in the cell though, for now the glow was almost continuing. He looked as if he were painted to phosphorescence.

"I've not far to go, Arthur," he said soberly, as I sat looking at him. "The energy which began in leaps has increased to a positive continuous discharge. Life energy—electronic energy—is flowing out of me like water down a sluice. In a myriad directions, in a myriad dimensions and spaces, images of me must be flashing, appearing, disappearing, shading off into infinite dimensions we cannot even guess at. See—look here!"

He laid his hand on the bunk and for the first time I saw that it was translucent. He was becoming as transparent as glass.

"When the last scrap of energy has exhausted itself, it will be the end of Mark Grayson, and thank God for it!" he said. "You have been my true friend, so do me a favour. Tell all you know about me to the Science Association. Hand them the notes you have made. They will perhaps believe. Tell them to destroy that machine of mine. Things like this are not for Man to understand until he has learned a lot more science."

With this I had to leave for my time was up. Then, four days later, I read this in the paper under big headlines:

MARK GRAYSON DISAPPEARS!

Dr. Mark Grayson, the famous scientist, convicted recently as criminally insane and awaiting entry into an asylum, was found today to have vanished from his prison cell, and there is no sign of how the escape was effected. It is presumed that it was accomplished scientifically because there is no trace of window or door having been tampered with. The police are conducting an immediate search.

Needless to say, the police never found him, and they never will. Obviously his last scrap of energy had gone, and he is at last untrammelled—or at least his great mind is.

For myself, I put his case before the Association and they have promised to examine my notes, of which this is a short history, written to disprove him the lunatic he was thought to be. I say that he was a genius, but before his time. As to whether my act of knocking him on that plate saved the world or not I leave you, and science, to judge.

Not that the last of his images has even now been seen. Electronic radiations still reproduce—or at least rebound—from the subetherial waves of matter, and only last night while out with my wife we both saw a hazy image of Mark for a moment on the other side of the street, which immediately vanished. They have been reported from other parts of the world, too.

Until the last state of unbalance is overcome, the

world will be forced to remember Mark Grayson, and for my part I want to see that the world shall never forget him.

SCIENCE FROM SYRACUSE

FOREWORD

There are possibly some of you who do not understand the real circumstances connected with the One Week's War, which left a devastated world in the control of implacable scientists. Some of you will likewise be wondering why there reposes in the center of newly built New York City a railed-off portion in which stand a few buildings resembling those of ancient Greece. Still more must some of you wonder why in a solid block of four buildings one is missing and gapes like an empty tooth socket.

The facts may be garbled in the proper record when it comes to be written, therefore the narrative of the scientist himself who caused the trouble is set out here. Recently, this record of his aims and experiences, written in his own hand, was released from official custody and was instrumental in bringing about his destruction. I was given the task of patching up the parts left unclear.

This I have done to the best of my ability. I am no journalist. I used to be a police officer—Officer James

Baystroke—until my mistaken notions of this scientist's greatness led me into other fields

That which follows is the record of the scientist himself, and you will find it, I think, a record unexcelled in history for its scientific implications and obvious revelations of a cold-blooded egotist.

* * * * * *

I am writing this record to reassure myself—if any reassurance be needed—that the men and women of this era are gullible fools. Or maybe it is their lack of scientific knowledge that makes them so.

For instance, I caused a tremendous commotion when I first appeared in Times Square, New York City, on July 14 last. To a certain extent, I can understand it. I suppose it did look odd to the uneducated to see an object like an upright glass coffin emerging out of thin air, gradually becoming solid, and then holding up a converging stream of traffic from all points of the compass.

I closed my energy switches and a side in my machine opened. My interest in the people, the buildings, the queer type of vehicles, and so on, was cut short by the arrival of an officious individual with a badge on his tunic and a peaked cap.... I could not understand a word he said. He did not talk my native Greek, so I listened in patience until his tirade was over—then I stated quietly: "I am Archimedes of Syracuse, situated in West Greece...." I repeated it over and over again in the hope that it might penetrate. I think my name

'Archimedes' stirred something in his unlearned brain. I could not expect much, after all. He was clearly no intellectual. He had none of my development of forehead, for instance. He did not even possess a beard like mine, nor the easy Grecian raiment.

After a great deal of pointless jabbering, he gave some kind of order. My machine was hoisted onto a truck, a process I watched with considerable anxiety; then I was motioned to sit in the truck beside it. I obeyed, and the very efficient young man in the tunic settled beside me. Then we started off for some unknown destination.

As we went, I had the opportunity to study the design and architecture of the city, very different from my own Syracuse, but not at all as efficient as I had anticipated. It irritated me to find so little real evidence of good use being made of my original conceptions of the pulley, hydrostatics, and so forth. That short journey did much to convince me of the poor brainpower of my new-found associates.

Finally I was conducted to a solemn-looking kind of building—but before I went inside it, I took the precaution of locking the switches on my machine. I could not afford to have inexperienced hands tampering with it. It had carried me this far through Time and might need to carry me yet further.

Inside the building, a man with a badge behind a high desk reeled off more unintelligible questions, and he seemed to empurple slightly as my young captor gave my name very clearly. But why dwell on the unreasonable actions of the men with the badges? They thrust me into a cold room with bars all around it. I was left to meditate on the decadency of what I had believed would be an advanced civilization.

It was probably a matter of some hours later when a group of men were shown into my cell. I was immediately impressed. All of them had keen eyes and good cranial development. I realized I might at last gain some information—or at least explain my own position to them. The hope was realized, when after I had greeted them, one of them spoke in my own tongue. He spoke it with slight differences and truncations, but intelligibly enough.

"I am Dr. Nathan, Professor of Ancient Languages.... You have, I understand, insisted on the fact that you are Archimedes of Syracuse?"

"I am Archimedes!" I retorted. "But nobody seems to understand my language. You are the first."

He told me—with some scepticism, I thought—that this was America, that the people used the English tongue, and the year in their calendar Anno Domini. He told me a lot of other things, too, which only served to confirm my preconceived belief of an unintelligent age.

"This is not—not a hoax?" Dr. Nathan asked me quietly, as I pondered. "Dozens of times a year, hoaxes are perpetrated, especially scientific ones, with the specific idea of gaining money from a gullible public."

Hoax! I, Archimedes, a hoax! I think I showed my anger clearly, for Dr. Nathan hurried to explain.

"Perhaps you do not realize how amazing all this is. You are supposed to belong to a period nearly two hundred years before the birth of Christ—and yet you are here! How did you do it?"

It was only then that I began to appreciate the bewildering fact that these so-called efficient beings of this future era had no idea of how to travel in Time. Dr. Nathan told me—and indeed later showed me—records to prove that historians had believed me killed in a market place by invading Romans while I was studying a problem marked out in the sand. If nothing else was developed, at least imagination was!

"I traveled through Time," I told my hearers firmly. "Is that so difficult to understand? My machine merged into what you call Times Square. Obviously, the orbital and axial revolution of the Earth shifted my position on the planet's surface, which explains my arrival in America instead of Greece. As to the scientific details—"

Dr. Nathan interrupted me. "The scientific details are very important, and for that reason are better explained before a gathering of the nation's greatest scientists. In the meantime, your Time Machine has been removed to the safety of the Science Institute. While your case is thoroughly investigated, Professor Archimedes—"

"*Counselor* Archimedes!" I scornfully corrected.

"Counselor," he apologized gravely. "While we examine matters, you will have every courtesy our social sphere can offer. If everything is genuine, all honor must—and will be—accorded to you as the greatest scientist that ever lived."

I could hardly credit it, but they still doubted me. I did not argue then, because it did not suit my purpose. I went with them to a place they called a hotel—extremely comfortable, I confess—and thereafter spent my time giving interviews to an interpreter who in turn churned out my words verbatim for the presses.

Then there were movie-machines, televisors, and other devices, which though intricate in themselves, had stopped far short of the possibilities I had visualized for them when first conceiving them. I saw all around me the real need for advancement.

But that could come later.

* * * * * * *

Evidently my associates were ultimately satisfied with my genuineness, for they asked me to attend a banquet of scientists at which I was to be the guest of honor. In two weeks that had elapsed, I had learned to speak the English language fairly well, and so was able to converse directly with most of the men and women whom I met.

Many of them seemed rather in awe of me, a fact I could well understand, since I realized I was considered the father of all the sciences. It rather disturbed me to find that some of the misguided newspapermen insisted on coupling me with a bath from which I had arisen without raiment to run through the streets of Syracuse shouting 'Eureka!' A gross libel indeed upon my discoveries of hydrostatics and equilibristic pressure.

At the banquet I was toasted and feted freely, and then was asked to explain myself. How had I crossed Time? I rose, choosing what words I should use to make myself clear to these so-called scientists.

"Space-time and matter are inseparably interlinked," I told them. "But while we move freely in space—realizing also that to do so we must also move in Time—we cannot imagine how to move in Time without encompassing the corresponding amount of space with it. For instance, you might decide that to cover 500 miles would occupy about an hour of so-called Time...but to cover 500 hours and use no space at all would, to you, seem to consist of being motionless while the time elapsed. Yet even then you would be moving in space on the earth's surface. Your own body would be giving off energy, moving forces. You would still be moving in space though not in any measurable fashion....

"To hurdle Time, therefore, without involving any great quantity of space, and to keep conscious while doing it, involves a knowledge of atomic physics. You know—from my own original postulation indeed—that atomic time, due entirely to relative smallness, passes through a thousand years or so whilst we of the macrocosmic universe occupy but a second. The different relative outlook and vibratory speed of the matter in the Macrocosm causes it.

"Once I realized this fact, I saw that my problem ascended into the realms of pure physics. What I had to do was determine the vibratory rate of atomic constitutions and duplicate that vibratory rate, thereby making myself, and my surroundings vibrate at a speed similar to that in the atomic world. I finally accomplished it. I found, with my body incased inside a machine embodying atomic vibrations, that I became, as it were, part of a hyper-macrocosm. Around me, ordinary time appeared a matter of vast hundreds-of-years leaps instead of the gradual procession of minute following minute.

"I had completed my invention when the Roman invasion of Syracuse began. I was studying out my exact mathematical theorem in the sand of the market place when I heard of the legions coming. I departed hastily—so hastily, indeed, that I had little time to determine whither I would go. I found when the Time-leap had ended that I had arrived here."

From the expressions of those around me, I could tell that none save the really profound physicists knew exactly what I was talking about. But I had told them the truth, at least insofar as the science went. I had not told them my exact motives for all this, because I did not deem it wise.

"There is only one drawback," I resumed, after a silence. "Time-travel is a one-way journey. It is quite impossible to move into the past, because the make-up of the physical world prevents it. One can only move futurewards, to a gradual and greater disorganization. One can no more travel backwards in Time than one can force an oak tree to return to an acorn. So my friends, I am with you until I choose to journey further into the future."

At that I sat down, noting what effect I had produced; a pretty strong one, judging from the talking that went on. Most of it was so rapid that my newly acquired knowledge of the language did not help me much. But after a while the Master of Ceremonies arose and bowed to me gravely.

"Counselor Archimedes, you are wisely named," he said. "And we consider it is our great fortune that you happened to pick our age of all the possible ages you might have landed in. You have, rightly perhaps, called our world badly developed—badly organized. You deplore the use that has been made of your original inventions...but at least you must admit that it is far in excess of the amenities of your own Greece?"

"To a certain extent," I replied pondering. "But such inventions as you have, radio, television, flying machines, automobiles, high-speed trains, and so on, are but devices which I urged my own men of Greece to use. My efforts to do it got me labeled as a necromancer. You have not, for instance, got a destructive ray amongst your armaments, such as I loaned to the hordes opposing the Romans? History speaks of a burning glass. Actually, it was a projector generating etheric vibrations. So you see, you have not progressed very far.

"In this age," I finished quietly, "I believe you will be open-minded enough to try new ideas—ideas which will straighten out your present haphazard conditions. For instance, I believe I am right in perceiving you all live under the shadow of war?"

"We live in an uneasy peace," the M.C. admitted with a sigh. "We have two great wars to our shame—and a third is not impossible, as what is known as the Fifth Power gathers momentum for the real Armageddon. To progress in face of incessant threat of war is not at all easy. But you, Archimedes," he went on urgently, "might well straighten out the tangle. After all, you are the greatest scientist of all time."

I do not think anybody guessed my inner thoughts as I replied.

"I will do what I can, willingly. Science must expand. Get me into contact with your present rulers and I will use my knowledge to your benefit. You have that assurance."

* * * * * * *

I was rather surprised to note the speed with which scientists and public bodies took up my offer of assistance. Within a week, I had interviews with the President of America himself. I was also transported to other countries to discuss with rulers, and there followed a series of conferences from which there emerged the decision to appoint me World Counselor. As the President of America himself said, when making the announcement:

"Perhaps what several unscientific men have failed to do, one scientific man can accomplish."

I did not regard his remark as flattery, but as a simple truth. Inside of a month, therefore, I was World

Counselor and was given a big executive building in the middle of New York to conduct my labors. My first step was to decide how to stop impending war with the Fifth Power.

I confess here that I had known right from the start what my decision would be, but for obvious reasons, I spent a lot of time apparently brooding over the reports of world conditions which were all diverted to my executive headquarters. When finally I made my report to the world over the radio and television, I am afraid I shocked everybody except the Fifth Power—for I stated that war was not an issue to be avoided, but to be faced. I told the people plainly that war—violent, brief and relentless—was the only true foundation of a new and lasting civilization.

As I had expected, this started a storm...but also as I had expected, the poor fools clung rigidly to the treaty they had signed which gave me absolute authority as World Counselor. The idea of breaking their treaty obligations when it suited them never dawned on them, I think. Nations had sworn to abide by my decisions regarding matters of progress—probably believing they would have an easy rise to peace and security while I did all the work...therefore, my decision that war was necessary pleased nobody except the Fifth Power.

I faced tirades from the President, insults from press and public alike—but such was my opinion. I was protected from actual physical attack by a perpetual strong-arm guard....

I had said that war was necessary before a real civilization could begin—but I had not said when the war was to commence. I knew it would be soon, for the avaricious Fifth Power was ready to strike the moment its strategic manoeuvres were completed.

Even from my own staff in the executive building, I faced a good deal of veiled invective—in particular from my third secretary, whom I was surprised to discover was actually the young police officer who had treated me so courteously on my arrival. I well recall how angry he seemed whilst upbraiding me for my decisions.

"Do you realize what you have done, sir?" he demanded of me, his young face flushed. "You've destroyed the trust of all right-thinking people! They put you in virtual power because of your scientific prowess, and the first thing you do is betray them! I love science, and always have done so, which is one reason why I gave up ordinary work as a police officer to become employed in this great organization. I wanted to feel I was helping along the birth of a new world. And what do you do? You decide to destroy it!"

"You are very young," I told him gravely. "Do you not see that a world must first be purged of all sources of disorder before it can really build securely?"

"I see that, yes—but there is no legitimate reason for ordering massacre and barbarism to accomplish it!"

I said, "When you realize that human beings are so many masses of electricity constantly accumulating to no purpose, you will have little compunction about destroying the lot in order to bring a better world into being. The world appointed me Counselor—and the world must realize that perfection only comes the hard way."

He stood looking at me, obviously distraught. Then he burst out:

"I no longer believe you give two hoots about advancing our age! Nor do I credit your seeming benevolence any longer! I believe you have some *reason* for all this—some scientific reason you've never revealed."

Just for a moment, I wondered if he had really penetrated to the exact reason for my methods—then I realized the impossibility of it. But I told myself, here was a young man who was not quite such a gullible fool as the rest. I answered him quietly enough.

"You are in no position to question your superior, Baystroke. Return to your work. And remember that whatever you think or do, you will always be watched."

He went out without a word. When I thought back on the conversation, it made me smile a little. So young a man challenging me! Me—Archimedes!

The greatest scientist that ever lived! As these fools would know before I finished with them. What circumstance had prevented me from doing in my own age should certainly not prevent me here. Of that I was determined.

My edict that war was necessary started a sudden increase in armament production and mobilization of man and woman power. I had fully expected that, and stressed constantly the necessity to rid the world of dangerous elements before a real start could be made. The idea seemed to impress itself on the people, and they actually began to see a certain virtue in what they were doing.

For myself, I made special plans. I discovered the best scientific engineers in the country and outlined plans to them—plans for weapons which, in the hands of the rest of the world, would have been asking for the Earth itself to be blown out of its orbit. Most of the inventions I had worked out were ramifications of the somewhat childish ideas prevalent in this age.

After all, I could hardly explain to ordinary military chiefs what was meant by pure atomic force, generation of negative potentials, space-warp, and similar devices—so I had to rely on the limited but fairly quick uptake of the minds of the engineers I engaged. I took good care to swear them to secrecy, too.

At work in special laboratories—ostensibly for research—they manufactured a series of machines utilizing the forces I have named, forces quite beyond the comprehension of the dolts of this age. When the machines were completed, I had them installed in the deep basement of the executive building, thereby securing immediate safety for myself, and my staff. Whatever violent course the impending war took, we were completely protected.

Somehow, though, the news of these inventions leaked out. The President demanded explanations. I made it clear that the devices were secret scientific weapons for our own use in destroying the Fifth Power if ordinary military and economic means proved futile. I think the idea of a 'secret weapon' convinced the President; it seemed that most past wars had implied, but never brought forth, a secret weapon. What the President did not know—in fact what nobody knew—was that the devices were for my use only.

As I had anticipated, I had only just enough time to complete my plans when the Fifth Power struck. Immediately, I gave orders to my trained technicians in the basement, and machinery came into action, causing the executive building to become surrounded in a deep violent glow.

Baystroke was the only one with me when the onslaught began. We stood together at the window watching the battle taking place in the air, listening to the whine of bombs and their shattering detonations. I think my unmoved, thoughtful expression as I surveyed the destruction rather upset my former young devotee. He swung on me with sudden fury.

"Counselor, you're a devil!" he cried, his eyes blazing. "Look down there—! A mighty city filled with fighting people—a city being destroyed, all to gratify your cockeyed notions on building a new civilization! So it is in probably nearly every city in the world. So it will go until munitions are exhausted...."

"Which will be in about a week," I told him. "Computation of war potential and munition reserves has shown me there will be a war of unparalleled violence for about a week—then peace through lack of materials, which I have cut off at every source."

"And you smile!" Baystroke cried. "Anyway, what makes you think we can last for seven days? We might be bombed out of existence any moment."

I nodded to the bluish screen outside. "Not while that exists, my petulant young friend. This building is protected by a film of force on all sides and above. You are aware of the simple principle of explosion? You know that atomic aggregates change their paths with such terrific speed that they blow their structure asunder? Well, this force-screen, generated in the building basement, throws a neutral current through any such tendency. Therefore, bombs dropped here will not explode. They will penetrate the screen, yes— but nothing more since they fall in between neutralizing curtains."

Baystroke shouted, "Then why the devil aren't our forces equipped with such devices?"

"And prolong the war? Make one side win? No.... In reconstruction, all parties must start equal." I smiled reflectively, "You see, when this war is over, I shall be the master of the world. That is right, because I have the greatest scientific knowledge of any living man— and the world knows it. If I find the war drags on too long, there are things I can do to hasten its conclusion."

"Such as?"

I shrugged. "I can use again the heat rays I used in Syracuse; I can release pure atomic force, adopt mind paralyzers. Do many things.... But I do not think it will become necessary."

Baystroke was silent for a moment, studying the

onslaught outside. Then he eyed me again.

"What gratification will you get of being master of the Earth, if there is nobody left in it to master, that is...."

"There will be some," I answered ambiguously. "Besides, mastery of the world is only the commencement of real progress—the dawn of the age I tried to establish in my native time and country, but was prevented by there being so many people against me. Here it will be different. Science such as I possess will reach out—can reach out—to the furthest stars...."

To my surprise, Baystroke turned away abruptly.

"Is it possible to walk out through this radiation screen?" he asked curtly, and as I nodded he went on. "I've seen all I want to see of Archimedes, the benevolent scientist aiming at setting the world to rights. I prefer to fight with my fellow men—die with them, if need be...and if I don't die, maybe I'll even fight you someday!"

"Your knowledge against mine?" I asked him pityingly.

He nodded grimly. "Yeah. Someday I'm going to find out just why you did all this...."

Before I could reply, he was gone, but I made a mental note that if this disillusioned young man crossed my path again, it would perhaps be better to have him removed. Of course, I had a reason for all this—but the time for its revelation was not yet....

For a trifle over a week, as I had calculated, the war raged—and it was surely the most terrific war ever staged on earth. Though I watched it daily, though I knew my staff in the building thought me completely mad but did not dare to say so, I was not particularly moved by the scenes of destruction and suffering constantly on the increase. Maybe it is something in my makeup. I have heard it said that the true scientist is totally without emotion—forever an implacable opportunist bent on progress at whatever cost. Perhaps that is my nature. I must confess that suffering in others has never stirred me.

Ultimately, the ammunition from every source ran out, as I had arranged it should. I gave orders for ambulance and rescue work to be carried out immediately, and began a gathering of radio and television news reports from different parts of the world.

Where is the need for me to detail what followed when those of you who survived know it full well? The war had gone according to my plans and had left a devastated world with no victor—except me. All that was left were masses of shattered cities and wandering survivors.

My deeper-laid plans came to the fore now. Disease was checked rapidly by the medical devices I offered; people were housed in temporary habitations. Then I sent forth a fleet of newly constructed long-range planes and gave them direct instructions to destroy every sign of armament in the world wherever they encountered it—and where they did not encounter it, they were to find out by any means they chose where war weapons were still hidden.

That I was master of the survivors in the world was abundantly clear—to them and to me. In most places I had cities re-erected in similar design to the previous ones as time passed by—no more than a matter of months—but in newly erected New York I insisted on certain changes immediately in front of the executive building. Here, rather to the surprise of the architects I employed, I insisted that four buildings be erected in precisely similar design to those in my native Syracuse—a solid block of four.

The completed effect of a block of Grecian build-ings in the midst of the newly erected city was rather strange, no doubt—but definitely necessary to my plans. Indeed, the buildings had hardly been finished, and left empty at my command, before that for which I was waiting took place.

Possibly quite a few people saw three more Time-machines similar to my own appear from the apparent air one morning in mid-New York. I saw to it that my comrades had a far better reception than I had, and gave orders for their machines to be safely put away. Then, after the city had paid homage at my behest, my three comrades and myself went into conclave.

In appearance I imagine that there was little to choose between us—nor will I waste time on names, except for Gralicus, the leading scientist next to myself. He was the one with whom I talked while our two comrades sat and listened.

"It seems your theory was right, Counselor," Gralicus observed, looking cut over the city. "We allowed the time to elapse as arranged—then as you did not return, we came to the same point as you ordered."

"These fools here thought I came by accident," I smiled. "They showed me some ridiculous legend about the Romans attacking Syracuse, and further showed me reports of a burning-glass attack invented by me. I traded on it by saying it was a death ray and instilled a healthy respect of my powers thereby. What they do not know is that I came here because an examination of future time-development showed clearly it was a good age in which to start the progressive action impossible in our own age and time."

"How true," Gralicus sighed. "We four are scientists beyond the imagination of such fools as those in our own time. To journey into the future and find a land wherein there is the material for active progress was a stroke worthy of your supreme genius, Counselor. And you have done well, obviously. The people are to heel."

"War saw to that," I murmured. "I had to make them fight in order to lessen the possible opposition. Still in the guise of a peacemaker, I had all armaments destroyed, so as to be certain there can be no dangerous attack at any time. Lastly, only a war and necessity for reconstruction could make it seem logical for me to reproduce our four most important Grecian buildings right in the center of this city."

Gralicus gazed down on them through the window.

"Excellent work!" he murmured. "And now—"

"Now," I told him grimly, "there is nothing to stop us. The conquest of the world is here; next we establish a dynasty in the greater spaces. I had those buildings made that way to obviate fresh plans. We know already that each building—as we intended in Syracuse until law stopped our efforts—is significant in itself, that each will contain special machinery—one, two, three, and four. The first for cosmic machines, the second for special radio work, the third for X-ray telescopic work, and the fourth for actual space-projectile work. Our machines will be better than those we tried back home. Fools though the people of this age are, they are excellent machine-builders. That I admit."

Gralicus said, "You plan then to contact other worlds, conquer space, master these other worlds with the scientific appliances you have devised?'"

"The realization of our dream," I breathed. "The domination of a universe by the greatest scientists of this or any other age!"

* * * * * * *

With my scientific friends to aid me, I was able to devote myself to more complex problems and leave the control of the people to them. Gralicus conscripted the people for machine-room work. He organized it so that the workers built machinery without knowing the ultimate purpose to which they worked. What they did realize, I think, was that to defeat our rule was impossible. It pleased me to see the dull apathy that attended their obedience to orders.

In the machine-rooms, the engineers built the sections of machines which I had devised. There were space-radio transmitters and receivers, etheric vibrators on a vast scale, destructive forces that could reach to the outermost planet and beyond if need be. Then there were astronomical devices of advanced design, cradlework for the holding of an advanced space-projectile to be driven by pure atomic force...and so forth. I planned to extract the ultimate possible benefits out of physics, astronomy, and mathematics. I planned to master space, space-time, and matter itself. How is it possible to put in this record the whole scientific detail, when none possesses such a brain as I to understand it?

I find, however, that this record is becoming a nuisance to me with so many problems on my hands. I will continue at a later date.

* * * * * * *

Some months have passed since I put down the record of my conquests. I return to my review of events with a rather troubled mind. For a reason I cannot understand, I believe the people of this age resent my domination—and that of my comrades. But why? Surely it is natural law? One master—one people?

No matter. They can do nothing. The first, second, and fourth Grecian buildings are now completed with machinery. I have inspected each one and am well satisfied. The third building, containing the X-ray telescopic devices, is almost finished. There are details to complete which will require the close inspection of myself and my comrades. The sooner it is done, the better, for the sooner can our conquest then begin.

Strange! I perceive Gralicus approaching the executive building, and in an obvious hurry too. I will resume when I know what news he brings.

* * * * * * *

Gralicus has brought disturbing news indeed. He tells me there are signs of active revolt among the people, and though there is no direct evidence of it, it would seem that my former secretary Baystroke is connected with it. I have little doubt that Gralicus will track the trouble down.

But time is moving. I have Building 3 to inspect. Gralicus has urged an early examination and is waiting there now with our two comrades. I will have to again postpone this record.

NOTE BY JAMES BAYSTROKE

SUCH are the last words Archimedes was ever destined to pen in this age and time! He imagined that by bringing a world to its knees, and that by sheer arrogance and scientific power, he could master a universe. Perhaps he could have done—and therein lay deadly danger. To defeat his mechanical ingenuity was impossible—but I, Baystroke, had not been idle, being aware for some time of the real ambitions of Archimedes.

During the War, the Science Institute containing his Time Machine was bombed. The machine, of immensely hard construction, dropped into the bomb crater and became covered with debris. Later, when with others I was employed in rebuilding the city, it was my luck to come across it. By night I and a party of friends spirited the machine to a group of physicists known to us to be in opposition to Archimedes' rule. We had a chance to study the machine in detail.

It finally became obvious to us how it worked—but it was also obvious that to perhaps attract Archimedes and his three colleagues into a machine and set them off into Time was next to impossible. They would be too wary. Yet this was the solution, I was convinced—for Archimedes himself had said Time was a one-way track. Therefore, hurled into the future, he and his comrades could never return.

What could we do?

We only found out when we were set to work erecting machinery in the Grecian buildings. We had noted how, on the completion of each building's machinery, it was thoroughly examined by the four rulers. Suppose the last building to be finished were naught but a disguised giant time-machine? At a casual glance, all advanced scientific machinery looks alike. We could probably erect time-machine apparatus and let it pass for astronomical machinery until close inspection—then it would not matter.

Simply, this is what we did. We found willing helpers in the machine rooms who duplicated the time-machinery on a giant scale. Others of us replaced the guards, and so finally we were ready. When Archimedes and his three men stepped into the building on that fated morning for the examination, nothing remained but to throw the remote control switch.

The building, the machinery, and the men inside it simply vanished—hurled some 4,000 years into a future from which they could never come back. What they do there is no concern of ours. We have rid the world of a grim danger, and therein lies our victory.

ABOUT "WHITE OUTCAST"

BY JOHN RUSSELL FEARN

As scientific knowledge advances, it is inevitable that the criminal will perfect his own scientific resistance to the probing of the law, but if, as seems the case, scientific justice must finally triumph, it will mean the reduction of crime to a very low percentage, the game simply not being worth the risk.

It is also possible, however, that with the almost total elimination of ordinary crime, there will come criminal activity of a type which will which will baffle even the earth's best scientific criminologists. Such a story is the present one, where I have imagined the Investigation Department of the future faced with a particularly strange sort of menace, and one which, given time and scientific achievement on this and other worlds, is perhaps not so outlandish as it at first appears,

In most of its main details this story follows out the fast-action tradition of the modern detective story, the one essential difference being the locale and scientific basis for the mystery. That the police of the future will control particular sectors of a city simply by switchboards is not by any means improbable, particularly as radio, television, electric eyes, and so forth evolve to their full possibilities.

Some readers, I suspect, will question the Jekyll and Hyde theory, which the story uses. So what? Strevenson started it off—then Arthur B. Reeves transplanted it into modern setting very effectively. Here it is transplanted into the future but with, I hope, the one virtue that a creature like the Outcast might be logically able to do such things by reason of his planetary upbringing. The idea in itself is not new, I admit, but the uses to which it is put definitely are.

Without giving the yarn away (because you may read this before the story), I am forced to stop right here.

WHITE OUTCAST

CHAPTER 1
THE ATTACK

The summer evening had fallen with quiet calm over Manhattan Island when the flyer suddenly appeared. On the less densely populated outskirts of New York City, families on their apartment roofs, either reclining or taking supper, saw the flyer first as a tiny oval against the crimson flush in the west.

Nobody paid much heed. Flyers of various designs were common enough over the rearing super-city of this advanced age. Only one thing seemed queer. The flyer was not heading toward any of the 2,000-foot-high directional towers that would guide it to the landing bases; and yet it was not lost. Its steady movement showed no sign of hesitancy.

Here and there men and women glanced at one another in surprise. Then throughout the entire block of apartments—known as Square 14—there was sudden consternation as the flyer came to a halt a thousand feet above.

Hundreds of pairs of eyes stared upward at a flat,

aluminum-coloured belly. A light of blinding amber winked momentarily within it—and then hell broke loose! Square 14—the entire vast cube-like apartment block—split asunder with a tremendous din.

Bricks, steel girders, black glass façades, whole roofs even, mingled with the shattered bodies of human beings in a blast that shook the heavens. Avalanches of debris thundered back into the streets a thousand feet below. The calm peace of the summer evening vanished with diabolical suddenness.

Here and there trapped survivors in the wreckage caught a glimpse of the mystery flyer as it swept downward. But now, suspended from its base, were twin horseshoe magnets—magnets that dove into the wreckage with ceaseless purpose, magnets of tremendous heaviness that hurled many a running figure into eternal darkness.

There was something incredible about the way those magnets plumbed the wreckage as demoralized human beings tried to find out what it was all about. For ten minutes the flyer darted about, driven with amazing accuracy, avoiding the stunted ruins that might have smashed it in pieces.

Then the magnets withdrew suddenly and the flyer whirled through the dusty haze, finally screaming to the ground on the top of plaster and gray boulders.

Arthur Corton, an uptown bank clerk, pinned under the wreckage by some miracle of fate, had his head free. He was possibly the only man who saw what happened. Through the dust he glimpsed an open airlock in the ship. From it a figure slowly emerged. He was almost naked, save for a loincloth; human in outline, but of a doughy white colour. His skin hung in pasty folds. His face was flattish, almost bestial, with spreading nostrils and eyes as colourless as glass.

Corton struggled frantically to free his pinned legs. Failing, he lay there gasping as the mysterious individual scraped hurriedly amidst the ruins with a tiny magnet in each hand. The man came and went with desperate purpose; then all at once stopped and listened.

All of a sudden he raced back to his ship at top speed, jumped in and slammed the door. There was a titanic gust of hot air. The flyer lashed forward with staggering speed into the murk and deepening darkness.

Moments later a party of rescuers came plowing through the ruins.

"Here!" Corton shouted desperately. "Here! I'm being crushed to death!"

The rescue squad asked no questions, got immediately to work. As it proceeded, Corton heard through his blur of pain the screech of alarm sirens, the blasting roar of stratosphere police planes, the distant crackle of static from electric guns slamming death charges into the upper heights.

Manhattan was prepared now—but the preparation was too late. The unknown craft had vanished utterly, and some seven hundred innocent persons were dead or brutally mangled. Then for Arthur Corton too the world was suddenly dark and quiet.

Between spells of coma Arthur Corton was afterwards aware of faces grouped round his bed—grim, determined faces, and one in particular which reminded him of a granite statue. He recognized the blunt, stern features of Vincent Burke, head of the Scientific Investigation Bureau's homicide squad.

Burke was speaking in his clipped, purposeful voice.

"You've been saying things, Mr. Corton—delirium, maybe; but if you can make it, I'd like to know more. Something about a ship and a man with doughy features—"

"That's—that's right." Corton breathed hard. There was damnable pain eating through his chest. In remote horror he realized he might never be sound again.

"I—I saw *him*—for a moment. About six feet tall, nearly naked, colour of wet bread—"

In jerking gasps Corton went on to tell of the magnets, of the searching.

"I don't know who—" he started to say, and then he relaxed and became motionless.

Burke compressed his lips and turned away, rubbing his heavy jaw slowly as his associates and the newsmen gathered round him.

"Exit the last survivor," he observed laconically, shrugging. "Come on, Sphinx, we've things to figure out at headquarters. No statement yet, boys," he added briefly.

'Sphinx' Grantham, his personal assistant, with features about as communicative as those of his stony superior, followed his chief out of the hospital. As usual, he made no observations. It was his job to answer, not to comment.

As the fast official car whirled the two police officials back through the traffic, the radiophone in the roof came into life.

"Calling Chief Inspector Burke."

Burke switched on. "Burke answering. Go ahead."

"Operator 9 reports further activity by unknown invader north of the city. In ruins of Square 14 again. Ambulance and rescue squads were overcome by gas and smoke barrage, but Operator 9 caught a brief glimpse of visitor. Six feet, white all over. Operator 9 took his aura frequencies on the detector. Invader got away. That is all."

Burke switched off with a gloomy smile. He glanced across at Sphinx' overlong, expressionless features.

"About the queerest set-up I've struck yet," Burke said briefly. "Sounds like an interplanetary visitor of some sort—but why the hell does he have to cause all this trouble? Why destroy Square 14 and all those poor devils?"

"I guess we're paid to find that out," Sphinx replied logically.

"Yeah—and we will!"

Burke broke off as the car drew up with a screech outside headquarters. He stalked through the building to his private office and snapped on the night duty button. In five minutes twenty men had assembled— trained, picked men, always at the service of the Bureau in the night hours.

"Now get this, boys." Burke stood facing them, his face grim. "We're up against either an alien murderer or else an insane man. If the former, he's the first visitor from another world, but that doesn't make him less dangerous; the opposite, in fact. We've got to find him!

"In this city we've brought crime to a low level, and no saboteur is going to start upsetting order while we're around! Seven hundred people dead—*seven hundred!* And all for no apparent reason! So hop to it, men! Contact stratosphere headquarters, contact Operator 9 and get the frequencies of this Unknown from him. Check everybody you think would have even the slightest bit of information.

"There's a chance that our killer is some crook in fantastic make-up using an extra fast stratoship mistaken as a space-machine. It's a possibility—so work on it! Get him—dead or alive!"

Without a word the men filed out. Burke turned and flipped a coin on the desk.

"Get me a packet of cigarettes, Sphinx. I've run out of 'em. Can't think without 'em—"

Sphinx took up the coin, then paused and tossed it back.

"You can't get away with that one," he observed gravely. "Better give me real money."

"Huh?" Burke looked up impatiently, studied the coin in surprise. It was not money at all; it looked rather like a badly scratched token of some sort.

"Somebody gypped me," he observed, thrusting the

coin back in his pocket and tossing over another.

Sphinx went out just as "Big Boss" Calman came in. Calman was the head of the entire Bureau, controller of every department, the brains behind the brains. But he knew the individual values of each of his chief inspectors, allowed them free rein unless circumstances demanded his presence.

"Everything set to go to work on this invader?" he asked Burke briefly, surveying him with his pale gray eyes.

"Yes, sir—everything," Burke nodded. "The boys just left, and I've plans of my own to work out."

"Okay—if you need me at all, don't hesitate to call. I'm going home. See you tomorrow."

"Good night, sir. If it's possible to get that killer—well, we won't be asleep at the switch, Mr. Calman."

CHAPTER 2
THE WORK OF A FIEND

For quite a while Burke sat pondering. Mechanically he took the cigarettes Sphinx Grantham brought in for him. He was still musing by the time Sphinx had come up from the night canteen with sandwiches and coffee. Then the radio bell rang with strident force.

Startled, Burke turned and switched on the receiver.

"Hello there, Burke. Listen carefully. This is Calman. I'm speaking from a public radio box. Come down to Intersection 30 right away. I have found something pretty queer. I believe it's the guy we're looking for—

What? That's what I said. He's lying dead among the girders supporting the 30th Pedestrian Gallery. Step on it!"

"Right away!" Burke closed the switch. "Let's go!" he added briefly, and Sphinx was right beside him as they raced down the corridor.

The fast police touring car whirled them through the floodlit and now almost deserted streets, drew to a squeaking halt under the mighty girders of the 30th Pedestrian Gallery. Calman was there, waiting by his car, the headlights of which were turned upward.

Calman said briefly, "Take a look!" and nodded his head.

Burke narrowed his eyes. A white figure, practically naked, was suspended motionless in the crotch formed by two immense X girders, caught round the waist. His legs and arms dangled grotesquely.

"Looks like our man," Calman said grimly. "I've been up to take a look. Come and see for yourself."

He led the way up the emergency stairway. Presently Burke stood looking down on that nameless thing so obviously dead. A gaping wound was on the forehead, from which blood still oozed in a dribbling stream. The entire figure, save for a loincloth of curious leathery substance, was naked. It was human enough in form, except for the ridged thickness of the skin. It was a skin utterly unlike that of a human being, rough and coarse as though afflicted with some mild form of elephantiasis.

"Queer how he got here," Burke mused.

Calman said, "As I figure it out, he must have been creeping along the Pedestrian Gallery above, slipped, and—wham! Anyway, it's the man. His ship ought to be somewhere around. I saw him hanging there in the lights from my car while I was heading home. Better have the boys look around for his ship, and we'll cart him to the morgue and see what sort of a being he really is. Come on."

Struggling and shoving, it took the three of them their united strength to lift that gross, heavy body. They managed it finally and staggered down the stairway with it, dumped it in the back of the roomy police car.

"I'll come with you," Calman said, withdrawing from his own car. "I've told the boys to take my car home. Let's be moving."

He slid in beside Burke and the engine roared.

Burke swung the steering wheel. Sphinx Grantham sat motionless in the back of the car, his deadpan face unmoved by the close proximity of the weird corpse. He gazed straight ahead at the swirl of lights as Burke stepped on the gas down the official traffic-way—90...100...125....

There were no limits on this wide, light-drenched expanse; a vast bridge, one of many crossing the newly created river dividing Manhattan in half where once Madison Square had been. Now Long Island Sound and the Hudson were united to facilitate watercraft.

Below, the river shone like molten lead. The girders of the bridge zipped past in trellises of mist. Then suddenly the front of the car was no longer there!

A terrific explosion hurled the hood skyward; flame and impact split the engine asunder. In two mad seconds Burke was aware of the slender rail at the base of the girders as it hurtled to meet the shattered car.

The machine plunged through. Flung clear, Burke went flying through space. Somehow he straightened his legs as he fell, went headfirst into the water and plunged below.

Dazed but unhurt, he bobbed to the surface.

"Sphinx! Calman!" he bellowed, fighting desperately against the current.

"Here!" Sphinx yelled, about fifty yards away. "All right?"

"Find Calman!" Burke shouted.

He threshed around, calling his chief by name. Sphinx swam level after awhile, blood and water trickling together down his face.

"Guess he's gone," he panted. "Lend me a hand, Burke. I got cut on the head."

Burke caught his assistant as he sank weakly. Though even their united efforts were feeble, they managed at last to struggle to the mud of the bank, crawled up, and sat there trying to get their breath back.

"He must have gone down with the car and the corpse," Sphinx panted at last, holding his damaged forehead. "I don't suppose the corpse would float out anyway; it was jammed pretty tight in the back. But Calman could have gotten free; it was an open car."

"Unless the initial explosion killed him," Burke said soberly. He gazed up at the break in the rail where the car had plunged through.

"That," he said slowly, "was no accident. Cars don't blow up in these days; they're fireproof. Either something was planted in the engine while we looked at that corpse on the gallery, or else— By God, Sphinx, I'll find out who's behind all this if it kills me!

"Calman's dead, and we'll have to get the dredges to work mighty quick if we want to save that corpse, too. Come on. We've got to report this. After that we'll attend to your bead."

Burke turned to stumble up the bank, then about-faced sharply at the sound of threshing water behind him. Something was struggling in the river. It came closer, visible as a man's head in the light of the bridge.

"Calman!" Burke cried. He plunged out waist-deep into the river again, helped Sphinx to drag in their almost exhausted chief.

"Thanks, boys." Calman staggered up beside him. "Hell, I thought I was finished! I went under with the car and my belt got caught. Anyway, I made it—"

Without further comment the three of them floundered up the bank, headed for the nearby radio box, and contacted headquarters.

"Well?" Burke asked grimly, as they stood waiting under the official lamp. "Any theories?"

"None that I'd like to express right now," Calman answered tersely. "Either this—this white outcast is dead, or he isn't. Depends on whether that explosion was timed for after his death, or whether the figure on the gallery girders was put there as a decoy."

"You mean there might be *two* outcasts?" Sphinx demanded blankly.

"There might be. Damned if I know the answer. Well, we'll see what happens next. If there are no more attacks on us, then we know it was a posthumous effort to kill us, and it failed. If otherwise, we'll begin a manhunt that the town will never forget!"

Calman stopped speaking as two spots of light enlarged into headlamps along the bridge. That was the police car they'd ordered.

The following day, as the broadcast media and morning newspapers headlined the explosion at the bridge and later commentators began referring to the 'White Outcast'—as the unknown marauder had now become known—three grim men at Bureau headquarters went over every detail of the problem to date.

They found no definite clue, however, for there seemed to be no motive in the senseless destruction of Square 14. The effort to destroy the three leading lights of the Bureau was more understandable—but again it proved nothing.

Was the White Outcast still alive—or dead? There constituted the main problem, and until the killer perpetrated some further act of mischief, the matter was unsolvable. Certainly there was no trace of his spaceship anywhere.

Burke gave the necessary instructions for the river to be dragged, and toward four in the afternoon the salvage was complete. The derelict car was removed to the official headquarters and the corpse jammed inside was dumped on the slab in the morgue. Dr. Rayfrew, the chief medical examiner, went to work at once.

"In the meantime," Burke said, "I'm going to take a look at that car. Maybe we can find out something."

"If you do, notify me immediately," Calman told him. "I'm going uptown to take a look into the Matthews case. You know where to reach me if necessary."

Burke nodded. He and Sphinx adjourned to the yard behind the building to survey the soaked, muddy ruin of the car that had nearly been their coffin.

"If you expect to find anything in that, you're a better man than I am," Sphinx commented.

"You never can tell—" Burke muttered.

He went to work methodically, tore out the sodden upholstery, stared at the utterly shattered engine. Presently he pointed to the remains of the carburettor. It was of the usual advanced type common to modern engineering.

"Notice?" he asked briefly.

Sphinx gazed at it earnestly, but he shook his head.

"So what? It's black around the broken edges. The fuel mixture must have caught fire."

"Yes, but *how*? A modern carburettor can't catch fire! An outside agency had to do it. Somebody arranged a spark of some kind that fired the fuel. The enormously powerful mixture we use went off like a bomb and— blooey!"

Burke went back to his labours. Finally he took out what remained of the metal front floorboard. Half of it, on the left where he had sat, was smashed into jagged remains. But the other half was clear except for a neat hole, perhaps three inches in diameter; a hole apparently bored by heat, for the edges were obviously blackened.

"Either I'm crazy, or—" He broke off at length, handed the sheet of metal to Sphinx. "Put this in cold storage somewhere. I may think of something later to match that hole."

"Crazy," Sphinx observed solemnly, "was right."

By the time Burke had finished probing around, Sphinx had returned. With him came the lean-faced medical examiner, Dr. Rayfrew.

"Say, Burke, you'd better step into my autopsy room. Plenty that is queer about that stiff you brought in."

Once inside the place Rayfrew nodded to the dead thing on the slab, then handed over a collection of X-ray plates.

"You'll see for yourself that the organs of this creature are utterly different from ours. Liver, heart and stomach are there, to be true—but not in places we ever heard of. Then the bone structure is different, too. Shoulders pretty weak, legs strong. I can't place it at all. As to the cause of death, it was probably cerebral hemorrhage caused by a terrific blow on the head. Perhaps the girder of the Pedestrian Gallery. It had to be a tough blow. This creature's skin is so dense, you couldn't hurt him by ordinary methods. Queer, also, are the main nerve branches.

"I believe he might be able to control the nerve endings of his skin, like a chameleon does. The skin has a highly sensitive undersurface. Probably got that way controlling the pigment. Perhaps, if his home planet were distant from its sun, a natural power on the part of an inhabitant would be necessary to make his skin supply these deficiencies.

"Well, anyway—thanks," Burke said, still puzzling. "He's a mystery. Was he the only one, or were there others? Where's his ship got to? The boys who think the pyramids are a puzzle should try this one! Well, let's go, Sphinx. I've things to do. Get rid of the body in the lethal chamber, Doc—no sense in embalming it for future use: may contain dangerous germs. And hang on to those X-ray plates."

Renfrew frowned. "The scientific community won't like that. As the first alien, they'll want to examine—"

"You've already done that," Burke snapped. "They can study your findings. Get rid of that body before it starts a plague!"

"Very well," Dr. Rayfrew nodded.

In his office again, Burke switched on the intercom.

"Terry? Hop down to the river again with the boys. Cover all the area where you dug up the car, send down relays of divers if you have to. Anyway, keep on dredging until you discover something that looks like a ray gun.

"You what? No, I don't know what a ray gun looks like. It's like a torch, I suppose. Use your imagination. It's only a hunch of mine, but keep on looking until you're cross-eyed, if you have to. Yes, I know it's soft ooze! Use hand and mechanical dredgers. Sift the whole bed of the river if you have to— Right!"

"This is absurd!" Sphinx protested. "Why a ray gun? We don't even use 'em yet."

"No, but I have an idea the aliens do. I figure it was a ray gun or something very much like it that fired our carburettor. It wasn't an ordinary gun, because the hole in the floorboard is too wide to show the passage of a bullet. A savage blast of flame could have made that hole."

"You mean a ray gun was fixed there, somehow?"

"Just what I mean. And since it wasn't found in the car, it must have got dislodged when the car fell in the river. Unless it was blown to bits in the explosion. But somehow," Burke finished slowly, "I don't think it was."

Sphinx Grantham scratched his head. "You got me," he said. "I—"

He paused as Burke lifted the telephone. He rang a number, the private waveband number of all wrist-watch telephones owned by agents of the Bureau.

"Hello there, 9? Burke speaking. Any dope yet?"

"Not yet, sir. We checked up on all likely crooks for their aura frequencies, but there was nothing doing."

Burke frowned. "So we'll try another angle. The Outcast is a mystery if he still lives. We're not dealing with a known factor at all. Start contacting the rest of the men in the Bureau and make your plans for finding his ship. I believe it ought to be around somewhere. Report to me if you find anything."

"Right, sir!"

Burke switched off, then on again as the emergency light went up. It was Police Officer Higson. His voice sounded excited over the speaker.

"Better come right away, Mr. Burke. I'm over on Sector 5. Something queer here. An antique dealer has been attacked by the Outcast. Come right away, or it'll be too late. I think he's passing out—"

"Okay. Get a statement from him. Be right with you."

Burke slapped on the office phone. "Tell Mr. Calman to meet us right away at Sector 5. No time to explain. Urgent!"

He glanced at his assistant. "Come on, Sphinx!"

They hurried into the waiting car. It swung around and bolted along the official traffic-ways at top speed. Neither of them gave a thought to a possible repetition of the previous night's outrage. It was the job of the Bureau to ignore personal danger—and they did, successfully. Nothing untoward happened.

They drew up on the other side of the city ten minutes later, to find a cordon of police keeping back curious sightseers from one of the oldest stores in this part of town, a section given over almost entirely to antiques of the twentieth century and preceding years.

Inside the shop, Officer Higson was kneeling on the floor with his notebook beside an obviously dying man. The victim spoke weakly, looked up as Burke came in. He was oldish, possibly sixty, with crinkly brown beard around a lean face.

"He saw the Outcast, Inspector—" Higson started

to say, but Burke waved him aside.

"What happened?" Burke caught the man by the shoulders.

"I—I was over there, at the desk. Things were quiet. I—I was busy—with my hobby—"

"Hobby? What hobby?"

"He writes messages on grains of rice and things," Higson volunteered.

"Miniature calligraphy, eh? You mean you were doing that when the Outcast came in?" Burke looked rather incredulous.

"Yes, sir. I—I hardly heard him come. Must have been watching me for—for he suddenly put out his huge hand and—and snatched up the grain I was working on. Then he fired something at me—a sort of dart—"

The man relapsed into momentary silence. "He stole my rice, my instruments, and—and ransacked the place," he finished dully.

As Burke puzzled, frowning, there came the approaching scream of an ambulance siren.

"You're sure it *was* the Outcast?" Burke snapped.

"I'm certain. Big, dirty white—only wearing a loin-cloth—"

The man sagged weakly, licking his lips. Burke stood up, scratching his head and watching as the man was lifted into the waiting ambulance. Then he swung around to the doctor in charge.

"Get Dr. Rayfrew from headquarters to attend to this man personally—nobody else. Tell him I said so."

"Very well, Inspector."

Calman came in hurriedly then, gazed around at the disordered shop. "What's going on here, Burke? Came as quick as I could. The Outcast again?" he asked seriously.

"Yeah—and he's no more dead than I am!" Burke fumed. "But the absurdity of the thing!" he went on helplessly. "The crass lunacy of the creature! He came in here and stole some rice on which that poor devil had been writing; also frisked the apparatus. That fellow does microscopic engravings for rings and things— you know, calligraphy. His hobby seems to be printing hundreds of words on grains of rice."

Calman nodded slowly. "I know the kind of thing you mean. But how did the Outcast get in here without being seen? Busy street outside."

"There are alleys at the back," Sphinx spoke up. "I saw them as we came up. The Outcast could have skulked around there and come up from the river somewhere. Anyway, we know he's alive—even if we can't fathom his motives."

"This," Burke said grimly, "is going to take more thinking than I'd figured. Maybe we'll get a lead when we know what it was the Outcast fired into that guy. I think it may have been a dart or something. Well, let's get back."

CHAPTER 3
EPISODE AT THE BRIDGE

The antique dealer died on the way to the hospital. Just the same, Dr. Rayfrew followed out orders and made an autopsy. He returned to Bureau headquarters with a grim face, entered the private office where Burke, Calman, and Sphinx Grantham were debating the problem.

"Well, Doc?" Burke looked up anxiously.

"Poison," Rayfrew said. "But no poison I ever heard of, and certainly not of *this* world! Introduced by a small splinter. Latent in effect, which was why the victim took a while to die. Guess that's all there is to it, gentlemen. I'll analyze the poison if you want."

Burke pursed his lips. "I don't think it signifies— All right, Doc, go ahead."

Burke looked grimly at Calman and Sphinx as the medico went out.

"Does it occur to you that we perhaps have a clue?" he asked slowly, after a moment or two. "This White Outcast is searching for something—that much we know. But doesn't his theft of microscopic writing on a grain of rice show that it is something small he's looking for? And don't forget he ransacked the store looking for God knows what. He used magnets when he blew up Square 14. That seems to suggest it's something metallic he wants."

"There's something else," Calman said. "The Outcast obviously got the dealer's name from the directory. He's listed as about the only expert in miniature calligraphy in the city. Only that seems to show that the Outcast knows English."

"Yeah," Burke mused and leaned back to think. After a bit: "He smashed down Square 14 and searched through it. Now just what was peculiar about Square 14? Same as the rest of the city, wasn't it?"

"There's one thing, but it's probably unimportant," Sphinx said. "It was the last Square to be built. Don't you recall the row there was over the brick delivery for the foundations? Clay pits went haywire or something and they had to import bricks from the Worth Clay Concession in the New Jersey section."

"Yes, I remember that." Burke pondered for a moment, then he said, "Sphinx, I've got an idea. It may be wrong, but anything's worth a try. I want you to get in touch with the contractors who built Square 14 and find out everything about it; where every scrap of material came from. Maybe we can get some idea then of what the Outcast is driving at. It should at least extend our field of activity, anyway. We're stymied as it is."

"Right!" Sphinx nodded, and went out without another word.

"Something else occurs to me, too," Burke continued, as Calman sat with puckered brows. "This Outcast possibly knows that Operator 9 recorded his frequencies on the detector. Next thing we know, the Outcast will try to steal that detector, or destroy it somehow. He might, to save himself from ever being found out."

Calman glanced up. "I didn't know you had the Outcast's frequencies. It ought to be a cinch now to—"

"It isn't, sir. The Outcast watches that. Even if he disguises himself, he takes good care to keep out of sight and out of reach of that detector. It would be safer locked away in our vault, where he can't ever get it."

"Well, you might do that," Calman agreed.

Burke made to rise, then glanced up as the door opened and Terry Walton of the Salvage Department came in. Without a word he laid a mud-stained, water-choked tube with glittering metal ends on the desk.

"Exhibit 'A'," he observed laconically. "This what you were wanting, Burke? We dug it out of the river just as you ordered."

Calman caught it up and stared at it. "What the blue hell is this?"

"Ray gun," Burke said briefly. "I'll look at it later. Keep it safe till I get back, Terry. Thanks a lot."

"You certainly work in a strange way, Burke," Calman commented, as they went down to the inspector's car. "Incidentally, where are we going now?"

"To pick up that detector from Operator 9. At the moment, he'll be at his usual station."

Burke started up the engine. In a moment or two they were cruising at a leisurely 100 m.p.h. along the official traffic-ways.

"Just how did you know about there being a ray gun in the river?" Calman mused. "That's pretty smart detective work, I'd say."

"Pure assumption, sir. I usually play my hunches.

I couldn't visualize anything else blowing up our car engine. There was a hole in the right-hand side of the floorboard, too. Being metal, only a ray gun—or something like it—could have burned through it."

"In that case, it must have been fastened somewhere near where I was sitting. Hmm—funny I never noticed it."

Burke shrugged. "Plenty of room to conceal it, and it was dark, too. Obviously it was put there while we dragged the corpse down from the gallery girders."

He said no more, and Calman sat rubbing his chin mystifiedly. The car went on, stopped at last in the middle of the great bridge where there reposed a base box: apparatus not unlike a railway signal box of old. There were seventy of these in the city, all told, from which the various operators of the Bureau controlled their particular quarter of the metropolis. They were in truth the police precinct stations of this advanced year.

"Shan't be a minute, Mr. Calman," Burke said, leaping out. He raced up the steps into the small building and found Operator 9 inside, busy as usual at the control switchboard.

"Evening, Inspector." He got to his feet.

"Better hand over that frequency detector, 9," Burke said. "There is a chance that Outcast knows about it and will try and get it. He may blow you sky high, even. I don't want to lose that record, whatever else may happen. I'll take it back to headquarters."

Operator 9 turned to the heavy safe and brought the delicate instrument to view in its mahogany case.

"Frequency reading is registered on the tabulator, sir. Safety catch is down at the moment. Release that and she'll jump right away when you come within six feet of the man you want."

"Yeah, yeah. I know all about it, son."

Burke picked up the case and headed for the door. Just as he passed through the opening, he fancied he heard a scream. He frowned, raced down the steps. At the bottom of them he stopped dead, as he came in full view of the bridge road.

The car was still there, Burke noticed quickly, but so was something else. A mighty figure of dead white, wearing only a loincloth, was standing intently at the bridge, watching something in the river below.

Burke's eyes narrowed as he took in the details of that bulky, doughy body. Without a sound he edged toward the car, keeping his eyes on the hideous creature. Instinctively he lowered the detector into it— when all of a sudden the Outcast swung around. Burke gave a little gasp. The creature was almost nauseating in appearance, like something fashioned out of white, clammy clay. The pale eyes stared with hypnotic fury.

"Get away from here, Mr. Calman!" Burke yelled. "Let me handle this fiend. We can't afford to lose you, too!"

Then, praying that Calman would follow his plea and duck out of the car, Burke centred all his attention on the loathsome white body. The pale cold eyes held him for a moment as though in a trance.

"Operator 9! Quick!" Burke yelled, breaking the

spell. Then he swung about with a gun levelled in his hand. But he had not the time to fire it. With an incredible leap, probably because he was accustomed to a far heavier gravity on his home planet, the Outcast leaped clean over the top of the low-built car and landed in front of Burke.

Simultaneously a fist struck the police inspector violently in the face. Burke went hurtling backward against the ironwork of the bridge. His gun went sailing into space.

Operator 9 appeared suddenly, brandishing two formidable-looking guns. Burke doubled up his fist and drove it with all his power into the leering face in front of him. The doughy features jolted under the onslaught; then Burke saw the big hands tugging at a little pouch on top of the loincloth. A splinter, coated with venomous red, came into view.

Sight of it spurred Burke to desperate activity. He squirmed free from the bridge rail, rained blows on that mass of white, dense flesh, even gained the ascendancy for a moment.

Operator 9's gun fired noisily—once, twice, three times. One bullet hit the ironwork; the other two presumably drilled into the Outcast, but seemed to make no impression beyond inciting the fiend to greater fury. He charged on Burke like a whirlwind.

Burke spun around, slammed up his fist, rocked the Outcast like a pendulum. But more than that Burke did not attempt. That splinter was no thing to trifle with! He jumped to the bridge parapet, shouting back to

Operator 9.

"Drive like hell—to headquarters! Take the detector!"

Then Burke leaped, just missing the Outcast's clawing hands. He made a neat clean dive and plunged into the river far below, rose up shaking the water out of his eyes. As he emerged he heard Operator 9 starting the car engine from above, could see the Outcast looking down at him from the bridge.

Slowly Burke swam to the bank, climbed up it. When he looked back at the bridge again, the Outcast had gone. The chief inspector smiled bitterly to himself and made his way to the nearest official intersection on the lower walks.

Burke landed back at headquarters looking bedraggled and feeling ill. He found Operator 9 already there, waiting, the undamaged detector in his possession.

"It meant letting the Outcast escape to follow out your order," the youngster said briefly. "I just made it!"

"Good man." Burke scooped back his hair. "You can get back to your post now, and notify every man to keep his eyes peeled. We know the Outcast is in the city, anyway. I'll take charge of this detector."

He swept the instrument up and went out to the Bureau vault down the corridor. When he came back into the office, he gave a start of surprise. A drenched figure was standing there, clothes tattered and torn, eyes gleaming with anger. It was Calman, physically unhurt, but in a pitiable state of attire.

"In a little while," he said slowly, "I shall get thoroughly burned up if I drop in that damned river again. So he got you, too! I leaped for it before he had a chance to ram a dart in me. I just let out one mighty yell to try and warn you, then chose the least resistance. Got out at the south end."

"Then I guess you didn't hear me yell," Burke acknowledged grimly. "When that devil loomed up before me, I didn't even glance inside the car to see if you were there. Well, anyway, sir, you escaped, and that's the main thing. By the way, Mr. Calman— that killer must have known somehow of what I've intended doing."

"I've realized that," Calman nodded, "and it's something I can't understand."

"I've got one or two ideas doped out," Burke admitted, "but they can wait for awhile. I'm going home for a change of clothes before I get busy again. Six o'clock now. Be back at seven. Maybe Sphinx Grantham will have got some information by then, too."

He turned impatiently and swung out of the office.

CHAPTER 4
THE DECOY THEFT

It was exactly 7:00 p.m. when Chief Inspector Burke returned. He found Calman absent, but the chief had left word that he had departed on an urgent mission with Dr. Rayfrew. Burke wondered vaguely what it could be.

Taking advantage of the brief lull, he picked up the

ray gun from Terry Walton's department and spent half an hour making experiments on his own. He came thoughtfully back to the office to find Sphinx Grantham lounging around, munching a sandwich.

"Well, find out anything?" Burke asked shortly, tossing the ray gun on the desk.

"Yes—but nothing of much use, I'm afraid. Say, I hear you and Calman were attacked by the Outcast this afternoon and—"

"Forget it! What did you discover?" Burke snapped impatiently.

"Well, I found out that, as I had figured, most of the bricks in the foundations of Square 14 were made of clay from the Worth Concession in the New Jersey area. It seems, though, that several men went to the Worth works and asked where the clay from a certain section of the concession had ended up."

"And they were told it went into Square 14?" Burke asked quickly.

"Yes, that's right."

Burke snapped his fingers. "Now get this! Something was in the clay of the Worth pits which the Outcast wanted. He found it had been used—at least, that part which he wanted—in the bricks of Square 14 foundations. So he wrecked Square 14 to try and find whatever it is he seeks. Remember the magnets he used?"

"It's an idea, sure. But who were the other people who made the inquiries at the Worth works?" Sphinx asked shrewdly.

"I believe," said Burke, "that 'the other people' was

probably the dead Outcast we found on the gallery. He could be made up to look like an Earthman, and he could adopt various different disguises."

"He could at that!" Sphinx whistled. "Then this other fellow who keeps attacking you and Calman and murdering obscure people—"

"He, I imagine, was the partner of the chap on the gallery, and for some reason did him in. I'm sure I'm right on that point. And so far, the Outcast hasn't found what *he* wants." Burke broke off and smiled grimly. "And we don't know what it is, either."

"Something small, hidden in clay." Sphinx mused perplexedly. "Probably something with minute writing on it, if the attack on the calligrapher is any guide."

Sphinx gave it up with a shrug and glanced at the ray gun.

"Find out anything about this?" he asked.

"It was the thing which set our engine on fire, sure as fate. The area of the beam—I've fixed it up again so it works—exactly matches up with the size of the hole in the floorboard. It went through the metal in a second, smashed the carburettor, with which it was in a direct line, and exploded the fuel mixture. It was so arranged that—"

Burke glanced up impatiently as the chief keeper of the safety vault came in.

"Mr. Burke—the detector's gone!" he exclaimed hoarsely.

"What!" Burke yelled. "You damned, confounded idiot! Didn't I tell you to—"

"Yes, yes—to guard it! I know—and I did! You put it in the safe, and I've sat there every minute myself, looking in the safe at intervals to make sure—"

"*All* the time?" Burke demanded.

The guard gulped a bit. "Except for an interval of about ten minutes when I was called to the checking room. Somebody was on the telephone and wanted the criminal record of Henry Walford. I was the only one that could give it. When I came back to guard the detector again, it had gone. That was just now. It's half an hour since I answered that telephone call."

Burke thumped his fist slowly on the desk.

"Did this person at the other end of the wire thank you for the record when you'd finished?"

"I don't remember it, Mr. Burke. I just reeled it off—and you know what those records are. Takes ten minutes or so to do it—"

The man stopped, astounded. "Good heavens, you don't mean I was drawn off to recite all that stuff and there was nobody listening on the other end!"

"Who," Burke asked slowly, "asked for the record?"

"Chief Inspector of Sector 20. Come to think of it, it struck me as rather queer at the time that he should want such a record. But—"

Burke whipped up the telephone, got the inspector on the wire. Sphinx and the vault keeper stood listening to Burke's clipped remarks. And the guard's face grew drawn with anxiety.

"—so you didn't, eh? Don't even know Henry Walford? Okay, that's all I wanted to know."

Burke lowered the phone. "Keeper," he said grimly, "the inspector did not ring you! He never even heard of Henry Walford. It was a great idea to take up your time and keep you out of your department—but nobody listened to your recital. And since there is a Henry Walford record in the files, you thought it was all on the up-and-up.

"But it was somebody else who asked the question! And only the oldest employees in this organization, like you and Sphinx and Calman, and I myself—together with some twenty-five other employees in other departments—know about the Henry Walford case. Somewhere among these thirty old employees is the one who rang you up!"

"But nobody but the Outcast would want to steal that frequency detector!" Sphinx cried. "You're not suggesting the Outcast is among our own staff, surely!"

"No, I'm not suggesting—I'm telling! How else could the Outcast know our plans so well! Who else but one of the staff could think up a trick like the Henry Walford record! Of course"—Burke gave a faint smile of triumph—"I fully expected the detector would be taken. It confirms a theory I'm working on."

He eyed the vault keeper steadily for a moment. "You can get back to your job," Burke said quietly.

"Yes, Inspector. I can't begin to say how—"

"All right; all right. Forget it. Now, Sphinx—"

Burke broke off rather impatiently as Calman came into the room.

"Burke, you'd better come along to the morgue.

We've just brought in a fellow attacked by the Outcast this evening. The police called Dr. Rayfrew and I went along with him, since you were away."

Burke followed immediately with Sphinx at his heels. The man in Rayfrew's autopsy room was pretty elderly, plenty knocked about, but still alive.

"He's all right," Rayfrew said briefly, "except for bruises. About the first victim to survive the Outcast, I guess—except you and Sphinx and Calman."

"I went for the Outcast with an electric gun," the latest victim panted. "That scared him a good deal. And hurt him too, I think! It saved me from getting a dart of some sort. What? My name's Bradshaw. I'm a scientist, an inventor."

"Are you listed in the directory of occupations as a scientific inventor?" Burke asked keenly.

"Certainly I am. That was how the Outcast found me, I presume. I live in an isolated, old-fashioned place near the ruined Square 14. I was in my laboratory when the Outcast broke in through the window. He spoke to me—in English!"

Burke's eyes gleamed. "Then what?"

"He said he had heard—probably through the television and newspapers—that I had invented a machine capable of producing long-range heat rays. That is quite true; but I invented the machine for peaceful purposes, mainly with a view to opening up the Arctic for exploitation of its mineral resources.

"I know plenty of warmongers on this world would like that ray of mine for destructive purposes. Well, sir, to my utter amazement, the Outcast said I had stolen the secret of my invention from his medallion, that it was one of his own twelve scientific secrets. He demanded I hand the medallion over."

"Medallion!" Burke cried. "So that's what he's looking for!"

"Naturally," Bradshaw went on, "I denied all knowledge of a medallion. Furious, he flew at me and I hit him. Then he pulled out a dart. I realized ordinary weapons were of no use, but an electric gun I had handy kept him away.

"Had I not been in my laboratory, I'd be dead now— Well, gentlemen, he fled. I summoned the nearest policeman to come and attend to me; I was pretty well knocked about, I can tell you. Then Dr. Rayfrew came finally, and Mr. Calman."

"Your home, then, is about ten minutes away from here by fast car?" Burke asked thoughtfully.

"About—yes."

Burke got slowly to his feet from the bedside chair.

"Mr. Bradshaw, it is evident that by a coincidence you happened to have made a machine identical with one supposed to be the secret of the Outcast— in formula form, at least. The secret of this machine, together with eleven other secrets, is impressed on a medallion. Hence, the theft from the calligrapher, in the hope that it might be there."

"Say, that's right!" Calman cried. "What else?"

"Sphinx found out enough to show me that this Outcast, either by accident or design, planted a medallion in the clay on the site that is now the Worth Concession. It's a comparatively recent site, remember. The clay the Outcast wanted had gone when he returned; it had gone into the bricks of Square 14. Result—the attack. Thereafter, a desperate search for the medallion and its twelve scientific secrets."

"Then where *is* the medallion?" Calman demanded. "Isn't that the next point? I think—"

"I believe I know where the medallion is," Burke answered slowly. "And I believe I can make the Outcast come and get it—this very evening!"

"You can!" Sphinx cried. "But—but how?"

"You'll see." Burke glanced around. "Mr. Calman, I'm requesting you to order all members of the Bureau who have been in our employ over ten years, to be present in the assembly hall by 9:30. There will be around thirty, including ourselves.

"You're the chief, so the order had better come from you. I'll produce the medallion, all right, and I'll so arrange it that the Outcast will be bound to come for it."

CHAPTER 5
METAMORPHOSIS

Those of the staff whom ten years' service designated were not at all keen on Burke's scheme, but since Calman gave the order, there was nothing for it but to turn up. Thirty or so employees—all of them who knew of the Henry Walford case—presented themselves in the big assembly hall by 9:30.

Calman was there on the platform. Around him were one or two officials, Sphinx Grantham, and Dr. Rayfrew. Burke arrived last by the rear door, looking very resolute and keeping his right hand in his pocket. He raised the other for silence.

"In this room," he said slowly, "are thirty-four people. I checked them as they came in. Every one is human—except one! I have publicized the fact in the last hour that the medallion is here tonight for the Outcast to come and get.

"So the Outcast is with us, and I warn him that I have the whole building surrounded by guards. But now I must make a confession. I have no medallion. In fact—I don't even know what it looks like!"

There was a tense silence. Calman broke the spell finally.

"I'm afraid I don't get this at all, Inspector."

Burke's voice was harsh with purpose. "The idea, Mr. Calman, is to make sure the Outcast is here. And he is. He knows we are right on his tail, and only by guaranteeing him the medallion would he be sure to come. Otherwise, he would probably have made a run for it before being caught and exposed."

Burke paused and walked slowly across the stage. Then suddenly he whipped his right hand from his pocket. There in his palm was fisted the ray gun with which he had been experimenting. He levelled the weapon steadily.

"All right, Calman! Stand up!" Burke snapped.

"Me?" Calman cried. "My good man, have you lost your mind?"

"Show's over, Calman. You're all through. *You are the Outcast!* And this ray gun of yours is the only thing your blasted flesh will wilt under! This—and an electric gun!"

Calman got up slowly, his eyes hot. "Now look here, Burke, I can stand just so much nonsense! This is absurd!" he exclaimed. "You're overwrought, Burke! Why, you must be seeing things!"

"Yeah?" Burke made a signal. From behind the stage curtains a technician emerged, carrying a frequency detector. Burke motioned him to hold it up.

The audience plainly saw the red register needle tally exactly with the blue frequency reading, previously recorded, as the instrument came near Calman. Indisputably Calman was the White Outcast!

"Aura frequency detectors never lie, Calman," Burke snapped. "You are the Outcast—and I've known it for some time! But I wanted to be absolutely certain. I found out quick enough when you stole a detector from the vault. Knowing the safe combination we use, it was simple enough, wasn't it? But you did not know I had put *another* detector in the vault with a phony number-frequency on it!

"The real detector was carefully put aside for an occasion like this. I had to manoeuvre things so I could get a reading without your being aware of it—and believe me, it took some doing. You made the Henry Walford phone call. You killed the *real* Calman on the night we found that awful-looking body in the Pedestrian Gallery girders. You killed Calman as he went home!"

'Calman' breathed hard. Suddenly there was a hoarse shout from the audience. Even Burke got a sick feeling in the pit of his stomach. For with a slow metamorphosis, Calman began to change into something revoltingly different. His features slackened and smeared, became doughy white. His flesh thickened oddly.

In four minutes 'Calman' had gone and the White Outcast—dressed in the lounge suit he'd stolen from the real Calman—stood in his place. Even the weird creature's eyes had gone several degrees paler by inner control of iris pigment.

"All right, you win," the Outcast said, without anger. "I thought I was a good scientist—but you're one better than me. Why shouldn't I admit it?" He sat down heavily, shaking his head. "I don't begin to understand how you knew."

Burke's voice was hoarse from the strain he'd undergone. "I didn't suspect you until Dr. Rayfrew said the Outcast might be able to control his nervous system after the fashion of a chameleon. He might, in other words, be able to metamorphose, to change himself, at will. Then Dr. Rayfrew told me of the possibility of extreme toughness.

"I figured out that an explosion—like the one in the car engine—would be unlikely to hurt you, Outcast, but very probably would kill Sphinx Grantham and me. It was worth your risk, anyway. The floorboard hole was just as I expected it would be had you had a ray gun or something similar in your hand. It would be hidden from my view by the darkness in the car.

"Well, I had the river dragged and a ray gun was turned up. If, as I suspected, you were the Outcast, you could not conceal the weapon in your pocket; because when you came out of the river, your clothes were clinging to you and the bulge would have shown.

"Since you were with us all the time we got the other Outcast from the gallery girders, you had not had time to fix anything in the car beforehand."

"How do you know that body was a so-called Outcast, as you say?" the alien said softly. "How can you be sure it wasn't Calman himself?"

Burke snorted. "Don't be a fool too, Outcast. How could Calman have been metamorphosed into such a revolting mass of flesh—even by you? There are still some things that can't be done!"

"Indeed?" purred the Outcast. "Well, I really must not spoil your fun. Continue, Inspector."

Burke bowed mockingly. "Thanks so much for your permission."

His voice grew harsh again. "Yes, I suspected you, all right. I knew that if you thought the frequency detector was in your grasp—which it was, in the vault—you would spare no pains to try and steal it, destroy it to make yourself safe. You did—but you took the wrong one!

"To make doubly sure of being rid of the two most likely to find you out—Sphinx and me—you continued your efforts against me when I went to get the detector. You got rid of your clothes somehow and metamorphosed yourself into your normal Outcast appearance. You looked realistically over the bridge at a mythical Calman who might have fallen into the water. You did the same thing when you attacked the antique dealer, I presume.

"By tonight I knew what you were looking for. Because of the medallion pretext, I made sure you'd be here. What I do not understand is, why you didn't kill off Sphinx Grantham and me with darts in the first place. It was your logical way out."

The Outcast smiled bitterly. "Too obvious. It would have thrown suspicion on me. What I really wanted to do was to become undisputed head without you two being in the way. Some time ago," he went on, "I was fleeing through space from an enemy, returning to my home planet. It became essential that I get rid of the medallion of secrets as quickly as possible.

"I came to Earth, marked the spot where I had buried the medallion, and went on again without anybody on this planet being aware I'd landed. When matters calmed down, I was ordered to recover the medallion, never to return to my world until I had done so. It contains secrets of war engines that I stole from this enemy, who was pursuing me. I was allowed one companion.

"We arrived here and found changes in the clay site where I had buried the medallion. My companion and I spent some weeks learning your language by listening to radio and television broadcasts. Then my assistant, metamorphosed to look like an Earthman, started to make inquiries. We finally discovered the medallion was probably among the bricks of Square 14."

The Outcast sighed as though in mild regret. "My companion was against ruthless destruction, so I killed him. Then I destroyed Square 14 but failed to find what I wanted. Even though, were the medallion lying in the ruins, my magnets would have dragged it to view."

The Outcast took two small horseshoe bars from his pocket and then replaced them.

"I had then to decide how best to find out where the medallion was. How better than as the head of the Scientific Bureau? They, in an effort to catch the White Outcast, might discover the medallion's whereabouts quicker than anybody.

"So, having studied Calman carefully beforehand in readiness for such an emergency, I took his place— killed him on the night you found my companion's body on the gallery. Calman's body I merely rayed out of being." He said it coolly, unemotionally.

"One point," Burke put in. "Why did you change back into your Outcast pose when you made your attacks on the antique dealer and the inventor? Could you not have done such things as Calman, made your search under the pretext of police routine?"

"I could, yes. But while you were around, I knew it would arouse your suspicions if the chief of the Bureau started doing that kind of thing. Better to do nothing that the real chief wouldn't bother himself about."

Burke nodded slowly. The Outcast went on calmly, in a matter of fact manner.

"I used my dead companion as a dupe, certainly. As I have already said, I tried to be rid of you and Sphinx Grantham without casting suspicions on my own bogus identity. Once I got the Bureau under my control without you two worrying me, I could probably track that medallion down in no time.

"I tried all likely people—or rather, I intended to. I only managed a calligrapher and an inventor before you caught up with me. I felt certain the inventor was the one because, according to newspaper reports, his invention was identical to the likeness on the medallion."

"These twelve inventions," Burke mused. "I presume that every detail of each one is on the medallion in microscopic writing?"

"Exactly. The actual machinery can only be built with the medallion formulae. Otherwise, we only know what the inventions are—without knowing how to construct them."

Burke said, "Had you told us what you were seeking, to begin with, we would have helped you."

"I think not." The Outcast shook his head. "Twelve engines of destruction would interest the war-loving scientists of this planet far too much. Such men could have become enemies of my own world at a none-too-distant date. No, it was better I found the medallion intact, with its secrets unrevealed."

He got slowly to his feet. Then suddenly he whipped

back his sleeve and rammed something into his arm. Too late, Burke dashed forward to get a look at the tiny splinter.

"For an Outcast to die when his mission has failed is surely logical?" the alien asked quietly. "I have fought for my planet; you for yours. Both of us, I think, have lost.

"You wondered about my spaceship. It is in orbit nine hundred miles from Earth. It can only come down when this is operated—"

He whipped an object like a watch out of his pocket, fiddled with its tiny instrumentation, flung it on the boards and ground it under his heel.

"I have sent my ship on a course that will take it into the sun. You will have to solve interstellar space travel for yourselves," he added dryly.

Suddenly he fell back into his chair, breathing hard. With a final convulsive movement he became motionless and relaxed.

Burke turned away quietly.

"Cigarettes, Sphinx. I want to think," Burke said, as they went back to the office. He flipped a coin on the desk.

"Okay—but I wish you'd use real money." Sphinx held up the dud coin for the second time in two days.

"Oh, hell—" Burke began irritably. Then suddenly he snatched the coin from him and stared at it; at the roughed surfaces smothered in tiny, microscopic lines.

"My God!" he gasped.

Without another word Burke raced to the autopsy

room in the morgue, where the Outcast's body lay. Rapidly he searched out the small magnets from the pockets. Instantly the coin clung to them.

"That's it!" Sphinx yelped. "The medallion! Even when he was near you, your pocket held it in, stopped the thing from contact with the magnets. Lord, if you'd only known! If *he* had only known! But how did you ever come to—"

"How should I know?" Burke asked quietly. "Dug up by workmen, I suppose. Handed around as a false coin, got into my loose change somewhere. I may have had it for ages. Funny as hell, isn't it?"

Burke smiled faintly as he gazed on the Outcast's dead face. "You know, the fellow was right in some things," he added. "About war-mongering, for instance— Never mind those cigarettes right now, Sphinx. We're going to the river bridge. I've something I'd like to throw over the parapet...."

ABOUT THE AUTHOR

British writer **JOHN RUSSELL FEARN** was born near Manchester, England, in 1908. As a child he devoured the science fiction of Wells and Verne, and was a voracious reader of the Boys' Story Papers. He was also fascinated by the cinema, and first broke into print in 1931 with a series of articles in *Film Weekly*.

He then quickly sold his first novel, *The Intelligence Gigantic*, to the American magazine, *Amazing Stories*. Over the next fifteen years, writing under several pseudonyms, Fearn became one of the most prolific contributors to all of the leading US science fiction pulps, including such legendary publications as *Astounding Stories*, *Startling Stories*, *Thrilling Wonder Stories*, and *Weird Tales*.

During the late 1940s he diversified into writing novels for the UK market, and also created his famous superwoman character, The Golden Amazon, for the prestigious Canadian magazine, the Toronto *Star Weekly*. In the early 1950s in the UK, his fifty-two novels as "Vargo Statten" were bestsellers, most notably his novelization of the film, *Creature from the Black Lagoon*.

Apart from science fiction, he had equal success with westerns, romances, and detective fiction, writing an amazing total of 180 novels—most of them in a period of just ten years—before his early death in 1960. His work has been translated into nine languages, and continues to be reprinted and read worldwide.